# T<small>HE</small> GATHERING

## P<small>REPARING THE</small> P<small>LANET FOR</small> A<small>SCENSION</small>

## D<small>ON</small> D<small>URRETT</small>

(Second Edition, August 2023)

ISBN: 978-1-4276-5456-4

WWW.DONDURRETT.COM

# BOOKS BY DON DURRETT

A Stranger From the Past

Conversations With an Immortal

Finding Your Soul

Finding Your Soul Workbook

New Thinking for the New Age

Spirit Club

Last of the Gnostics

Ascension Training

The Way

Team Creator

The Path Forward

Get Healthy / Stay Healthy

America's Political Cold War

Post America: A New Constitution

The Demise of America

Evolve is the mystery, love is the key,
Evil is the history, live to be,
Hate is the pain that saddens the heart,
Hearsay is the heresy that kills love before it starts.

We are the ones, we have always been,
We were too afraid to stand, now we fear not to,
Time has taken over, love is on the rise,
The fire burns in our hearts and
light shines from our eyes.

Stand united as the darkness falls away,
Stand strong in heart and love never fades away,
Stand for love or fall into the trap
of ignorance and greed,
A journey of no return, what you
sow you will always reap.

Time to help awake those still asleep,
Help them see their dreams are
more true than fear,
Help them to their hearts and
keep their minds clear,
We do this with a laugh, a smile
and loving honest cheer.

So raise a glass of mead like the old times,
Sing and dance as the darkness revives its crimes,
Let the love in your heart shine,
and all will be fine.

– *Tor Webster*

# CONTENTS

# Introduction

This book is a fictional story, although many of the events depicted are close to the truth. For instance, the title of this book is a real event. There is a gathering taking place today. This gathering is occurring because advanced souls have been called to volunteer in what can only be called project Earth Awaken. These advanced souls would normally avoid a planet such as Earth that is mired in negativity and spiritual ignorance. In fact, many of them are so highly evolved that they would never even have considered coming to this planet at this time. But they are here. They came to help, because of the calling.

We are in the process of transforming this planet from one of very little spiritual awareness to one that is highly evolved, a process that is extremely rare in the cosmos. In fact, this is perhaps the biggest leap in spiritual awareness that a planet has ever undertaken as a complete civilization. This awakening could not happen without help, and that is why the gathering is taking place.

Perhaps I should back up a bit and explain how this calling went out. Sometime in our past, the DNA of humanity on Earth was modified nefariously by extraterrestrials (from my understanding). At that time, humanity was using twelve strands of DNA instead of two. We were aware of our inherent divinity and our direct connection with the Creator. This was the time of Lemuria and early Atlantis. It was a period of harmony and utopia.

When our DNA was modified, it severely limited access to our soul and divine connection. It set up a period of spiritual ignorance that has lasted until today. The ramifications have been a long history of war and violence that still continues.

This is going to be hard to believe, but at that time, a plan was put in motion (from my understanding) to repair our DNA back to twelve strands. It was recognized then that our twelve strands could not be repaired in a short time. In fact, it was estimated that the process would take approximately 100,000 years. And, it was also recognized that we might fail.

For the first 98,000 years or so, not much changed. Then Jesus came and put in motion the final act. He came to give humanity a push in the right direction. Many of the early Gnostics (Gnosis means knowledge, and a Gnostic is someone who has direct knowledge of God), especially the Cathars,[1] understood what Jesus came to teach. Likewise, many in the East already understood the messages he shared. But as the Catholic Church became dominant, the true teachings were suppressed. Gnostics were frequently killed as heretics, and not a small number were burned at the stake by Catholic inquisitors. The written words of the Gnostics were also burned and destroyed. The knowledge of a direct connection with God the Creator languished.

Then in the 19th century, spirituality began to awaken, and metaphysical practices began to appear in the West. The term spiritualism was born. This was mainly practiced by a tiny portion of the population, who became intrigued by the soul's connection to other dimensions. Spiritualism continued to expand in the 20th century, leading to the appearance of many people channeling spirits from the other side. This included Edgar Cayce in the 1930s and Jane Roberts in the 1960s. These channelings began to teach the world the truth about our soul and true heritage. Then in 1987, the Harmonic Convergence occurred, and large numbers of people began to awaken to the truth about the soul. The final wave began. This is when the volunteers began to appear. Most of them have stayed out of the public eye doing spiritual work and holistic healing that is raising the vibration of the planet.

What nearly all of the volunteers have in common is that they are Gnostics. They *know* that their soul exists and that it provides

---

1    A group of Gnostics who lived in Southern France until the 13th century.

a divine eternal consciousness that makes them one with God. This *knowing* makes them unusual and to a large degree outcasts. For, they can't exactly go around telling people that they are literally divinity incarnate. The volunteers are forced to share their awareness and spirituality in ways that are somewhat hidden from the mainstream. This book was written to show how they share their spiritual knowledge and how they are the unknown heroes who are saving this planet from destruction. To illustrate the work being done by the volunteers, I describe the journeys of several. These stories are fictional, although some of the details are based on the lives of real volunteers who I have met along the way.

I don't know the exact number of souls who have volunteered to incarnate at this time to help with project Earth Awaken. But the total is likey in the millions. I do know that I am one of them and a good source to write this book.

*   *   *   *   *

This book was written for those who have already begun their spiritual journey and are collecting information for their spiritual awareness and spiritual growth. I have made assumptions that you have already been exposed to many metaphysical concepts, such as Gnosticism, reincarnation, and ascension. If this is your first metaphysical book, I recommend that you first read *A Stranger from the Past* or *Last of the Gnostics*, two of my earlier books.

My purpose for writing this book is to share information. For this reason, I feel it would be useful to briefly explain what this book is about. The first part is about how we choose our lives prior to our incarnation. Not only do we choose our lives, but we choose our personalities and traits. These are chosen for a specific purpose so that we can accomplish our life's goal. Quite often, we go astray from accomplishing our goal, and I will demonstrate how that can happen and will show you how we can get back on our desired path.

The second part of the book attempts to reveal the near future and what we can expect. And the final part of the book, actually the last chapter, is about ascension. I strongly believe that we are living in a time of wonder, during which people will literally ascend to a higher dimension. One day someone you know will be here, and the next, they will be gone. They will literally disappear. So, while you may think you are reading fiction, I think most of this book is closer to non-fiction.

One final point about ascension. The scenario that I use in the last chapter is food for thought. No one can know exactly how ascension will unfold, and I am sure that I do not know. I provide you with one possibility, and you can use your imagination for what you expect. I do believe that a New Earth exists as a 5th dimensional planet, and that many of us will end up there.

*Don Durrett   8/11/2023*

# Chapter One

# IT BEGINS

Sampson appeared before Mestos. Immediately Mestos could read Sampson's energy and knew something was amiss. He waited for Sampson to convey the issue. They did not speak, but instead used telepathy. Their bodies were made of light and radiated a translucent energy. Both wore white flowing robes, but these were an illusion. Nothing on this plane of reality was physically real. Everything was made of energy and easily created with the mind.

Sampson began communicating directly to Mestos using his mind. "Our fears have manifested. The DNA has been manipulated on Earth. They have lost their conscious connection to their soul. Only two strands are now active."

Mestos did not reply, but merely nodded in contemplation. He had known this outcome was likely and had been planning for it.

"Mestos, as we are both aware, the most likely outcome is that they will destroy their planet."

"Sampson, we must do everything that we can to prevent that."

"How do you want to proceed?"

"We can help them to restore their DNA to twelve strands, which will restore their conscious connection to their soul. That is the only way to save Earth's civilization from destroying themselves."

Sampson was stunned. "The entire civilization? How can it be done?"

"By raising the vibration of the planet. We will use the same method we have always used. We will infiltrate the planet with advanced souls who can impact humanity and raise the vibration."

"How long will it take?"

"I have projected the possibilities and, considering free will, it will take about 100,000 years."

Sampson sighed. "That is going to be very difficult. Do you think we can succeed?"

"Yes, that is our only option."

"Mestos, this will require an enormous effort and millions of volunteers. I can't think of a project of this magnitude ever attempted."

"Nor I, Sampson. But if we don't succeed, they will destroy their civilization. We can't allow that outcome. It will impact the entire universe."

Sampson did not reply as he contemplated what needed to be done.

Mestos had already decided on a plan of action. "Form a council to construct a plan to restore their DNA. I will give you my input after I study the future timelines in more detail."

Sampson nodded, and then his etheric body slowly disappeared.

\*　\*　\*　\*　\*

Mestos and Sampson were discarnate souls who existed on the 9th dimension. To say they were advanced souls would be an understatement. At this level of existence, the souls were literally gods. They did not have a leader at this level, but if there was one, Mestos would probably be it.

At this level, their lives were spent helping to create and manage universes. It was a complicated job because of the existence of free will. These souls had to decide and determine how they would intercede in the creation and evolution of life itself.

In some respects, they were consultants, giving advice to less evolved souls who were pursuing creation. But they were also auditors, who oversaw the various universes for disharmonious events and choices. It was their job to prevent problems from escalating or impacting others. The Creator could always intercede, but these souls were given the opportunity to use their creativity to harmonize the universes.

In essence, the less evolved souls tended to create a mess using their free will. The Creator would step in and hit the reset button if events got out of hand. The beings on the 9th dimension of existence were the buffer group who could help a civilization from destroying themselves. In other words, the Creator did not leave us without any help for finding our way. Each incarnated soul had at least one spirit guide, along with a higher self, to help them navigate through life. In addition to this, there were many other discarnate helpers and guides who helped civilizations find their way.

* * * * *

Sampson arranged a council. It consisted of twelve discarnate beings, all of whom existed on the 9th dimension. These were the elite: the most evolved and distinguished he could find. They had all been informed of the purpose of the council and the events that had taken place on Earth.

They sat at a circular table. It was manifested instantly to seat twelve people. They all wore similarly manifested robes, which appeared translucent if you looked closely. Mestos opened the meeting using telepathy. "Welcome, and thank you for coming. What we are undertaking has never been done before, but I think it is our only choice."

He stopped and waited to see if anyone disagreed with this course of action.

"Mestos, I think we all agree that this is a noble undertaking, and we would like to see it succeed. However, the magnitude has some of us concerned. The number of generations involved is substantial. This will require thousands and thousands of generations."

Mestos nodded. "Indeed, I know what I am asking. We could do nothing and watch as they destroy themselves. Does anyone here really want to do that?"

Mestos waited but there was no reply. "It is agreed we must do something. I think we can succeed in raising their vibration over thousands of generations and then reaching a critical mass of enlightenment."

"What is your plan, Mestos?" One of the souls asked using telepathy, their only form of speaking.

"It is simple. It is the same plan we have used successfully many times before. We infiltrate the planet with evolved souls who impact society through sharing their spiritual awareness."

"But Mestos, we have never tried to do this before to an entire planet. To change their DNA, they will have to raise their vibration significantly. You will need at least five percent of the planet to become enlightened, and maybe more to reach critical mass."

"We have done it several times on a smaller scale," Mestos replied. "There is no difference. It will just take a lot of persistence, and a lot of effort."

Again there was silence.

Mestos was asking them to try something that had never been tried before. They had to agree with his logic: it was possible. No one could make a concrete argument that it was impossible. It was just the magnitude that had them concerned. The degree of work and the time required would both be enormous.

"Mestos, I know we have all thought of this, but I think it should be stated. To raise the vibration to the level required to restore their twelve strands of DNA is nearly impossible. Humans with only two strands of DNA find it extremely difficult to connect with Source and become enlightened. It is going to take thousands and thousands of years to raise the vibration of the planet. To reach even one percent of the population as enlightened will take thousands of years."

Mestos nodded. "It will take 98,000 years, by my estimation, for one percent to become enlightened. Initially, we will not have much success. However, once we reach one percent, we can begin to make progress. At that point, we can send a Christ figure who will propel awareness forward. My projections are that once the Christ figure appears, it will only take another 2,000 years to reach critical mass. In fact, once we get to two percent, we can have a harmonic convergence and send rays of love to the planet. This will help activate dormant parts of their DNA and awaken many more souls. At that time, we can send a cadre of volunteers who can make steady progress towards our goal."

After Mestos stopped, the energy in the room changed. All of the twelve beings became excited and glowed a brighter hue from their confidence.

"A Christ figure?" one of the beings asked. "What religion are you thinking of using?"

"There are a few scenarios to consider. I've checked many timelines, and the most likely is that he will create a new religion. We have a lot of time before we have to decide. We need to wait and see how the first 98,000 years unfold."

The other eleven beings nodded in agreement. Their nods signified that they agreed with Mestos' plan.

"If this works, Mestos," said a member of the council, "many of them will ascend to the 5th dimension. And if they ascend together as a group, this event could manifest a new Earth."

Mestos nodded. "That is the preferred outcome, and the one I'm hoping we achieve. Once enough souls attain enlightenment, the planet will reach a critical mass, whereby they can ascend as a group. From my projections, I think that as many as two hundred million souls could ascend if we are successful. Most of them will ascend together in the first wave."

There was silence as everyone contemplated the possibility. This had never happened before on such a large scale, but it was possible. And if it worked, it would be a most wondrous event. They realized that it was something that they should at least attempt.

"I think we are ready to proceed," Mestos said.

No one replied, which signified a yes response from the council. Mestos' body quickly disappeared, and the council dispersed.

\* \* \* \* \*

Approximately ninety-eight thousand Earth years later, which to them was like a blink of an eye, the same council sat around another circular table. It was exactly the same group, and if you asked them how long it had been since their last meeting, they could not tell you, because the concept of time works differently on the spiritual dimensions. It is as though everything happens simultaneously. Souls on these higher planes select the timeframe in which to meet. Sometimes they meet without any timeframe at all – outside of chronological time.

Mestos was wearing a golden-colored robe. It had long sleeves and nearly covered his entire body, from his neck down to his feet. His face was humanoid, although his eyes were larger, and his nose and ears were much smaller than those of typical humans. He also lacked any body hair. They did not eat food on this plane of existence, so his mouth and thin lips were only for show. The others also had humanoid faces and wore similar manifested apparel.

"Our plan has gone well," Mestos began, "and it is time to progress further. Now is the time to put everything in motion for the final outcome. I propose that we send Sananda to Earth to be the Christ figure. There is a highly evolved family in Judaea who have already incarnated to help him.

"His grandmother, Anna, has had several children who will make his goal obtainable. Anna's oldest son, Joseph of Arimathea, is highly evolved and is ready to help. Joseph has a shipping business and is highly successful and respected. He will be Sananda's mentor and guardian. Anna, who will be his grandmother, and Mary, Sananda's mother, are also highly evolved. In fact, we have sent several evolved souls to be part of this family, including his cousin John the Baptist, who will play a pivotal role.

"They are all Essenes and Gnostics.[2] The local religion is Jewish, which they will break away from and form a new religion, which will become known as Christianity."

Mestos stopped and waited for the first response.

"What will be Sananda's incarnate name?"

"Yeshua Ben Joseph, from the house of David. He will have royal blood. After he is crucified, he will be known historically as Jesus."

"How much of Sananda's soul will be infused into his body?"

"About half."

The room was quiet, but the agitation and intrigue was palpable for all to feel. Everyone in the room was aware of the magnitude of this decision. Sananda was already an ascended master, so to incarnate with that much of his soul would be like bringing a god down to Earth. His abilities would be superhuman.

"Mestos, I don't want to question your judgment, but I need to state what we are all thinking. First, you put in motion this plan to raise the vibration of the planet to the point where civilization could regenerate their DNA to twelve strands. Now you are

---

2    The definition of a Gnostic is simple: a direct connection to God. Gnosis means knowledge, and a Gnostic has direct knowledge of God. A true Gnostic lives by knowing and not by faith. Thus, a Gnostic does not get his or her beliefs from a doctrine or a book. Instead, their beliefs come from within and from experience. A Gnostic develops their own belief system and follows their own spiritual path. There are no formal churches or ministers for this group, although it is not uncommon for some to attend a local Christian or Unitarian Church.

asking us to put an ascended master on Earth whom very few will comprehend."

"Sananda is going to bring love to the planet," Mestos replied. "His mission will not be to succeed during his lifetime. For this reason, initially very few people will comprehend his teachings. In fact, they will get most of it wrong. The religion that will arise will be based on many fallacies and falsehoods. Jesus' teachings will be manipulated and misinterpreted by the leaders of the Christian Church for power and control. The beliefs of this new Christian religion will be so counter to the truth that over time it will become more and more apparent that they are not based on the original teachings. However, we will keep his true teachings alive and they will eventually supersede Christianity. This will take approximately 2,000 years."

There was silence as everyone contemplated this plan.

"Mestos, that is brilliant," one of the council members said. "Since civilization will not be ready for Yeshua's true teachings, we ensure that they are not lost. With our guidance and volunteers, we will keep his true teachings alive to a small group of people. These volunteers and Gnostics will keep this knowledge alive until everyone is ready."

Mestos nodded. "Then after about 2,000 years, we bring his true teachings back and reveal the truth. Everyone will recognize that his true teachings were there all along, but that the Christian Church had undermined and hid the truth. There will be a mass exodus away from the false teachings of the Church to the true teachings of Christ."

Mestos stopped and scanned the table.

"Mestos, I think I can speak for everyone and say this is an excellent plan. We support you and will do what is necessary."

The rest of the souls on the council nodded in unison.

\* \* \* \* \*

A short time later, Mestos and Sampson met to begin planning.

"Sampson, I need you to begin sending more volunteers to Judaea. We need to create several Gnostic groups that will keep his message alive. After Yeshua is crucified, it is important that his true message does not die. It can die out after a period of time as long as it is enmeshed in history. We can bring it back to life a few decades before the final objective."

"What about Christianity? Do we need volunteers for that?"

"Not very many," Mestos replied. "Christianity will evolve on its own. It will be more of a political religion than a spiritual one."

Sampson nodded. "I will work closely with the volunteers and their spirit guides to begin planning."

Mestos nodded his approval. I say 'his', but souls did not have a gender at this level of existence.

"I will plan out thousands of lives who will incarnate as members of these various Gnostic groups. How many years should these groups exist?"

Mestos hesitated. "Let the team use their creativity. There should only be about a dozen groups, and most of them should die out shortly after Yeshua's crucifixion. They can let perhaps three groups linger for at least a thousand years. At some point, the new Christianity will wipe out the last Gnostic groups. Make sure that the last group has a very strong connection to Yeshua's family. Perhaps make them descendants of Mary Magdalene. She should be a central character in this final group, because of her connection to the divine feminine. I would like this last group to be highly respected martyrs, who are the epitome of Gnostic spirituality."

Sampson nodded. "I understand. That won't be difficult to engineer. I think Southern France would be a good location. We can send Mary Magdalene there after Jesus' crucifixion. We can tie this group closely to both Mary Magdalene and Jesus' true

Gnostic teachings. This way people will have a group that they can connect back to Jesus. I will make sure there are enough volunteers to maintain their history. When we get close to the culmination of Earth's awakening, there will be plenty of history to link this Gnostic group back to Jesus. The historical record will not be lost."

"That sounds perfect, Sampson. For there to be an awakening, people will need to believe that Jesus taught Gnostic spirituality. There needs to be a strong historical record to this last Gnostic group. Have them last as long as possible, perhaps until the 13th century. If they get influential enough, it's possible they will be wiped out by the Catholic Church in a holy crusade. I like the idea of linking them strongly to Mary Magdalene in Southern France. Make sure that their teachings are true. That is critical. Their truth should reveal Jesus' true message. Then as the truth of Gnosticism becomes more and more known, this knowledge of a oneness with mankind, and a direct link with God, will be sought out and cherished. The awakening will start slowly, but then it will gather momentum as the truth spreads."

"It's a beautiful plan, Mestos. After individualism and materialism begin to falter, people will begin to look for something new. Not just socially and economically, but also spiritually. They will inevitably seek out the truth of their existence. At that time, we will provide a trail back to Jesus and the Gnostics, and people will finally be able to let go of their false beliefs of separation and mortality. They will awaken to the truth."

Mestos smiled. "Yes, just make sure that the trail back to the Gnostics is strong. Don't make it too difficult for the volunteers, the trailblazers, to recognize what the Gnostics left behind. We want Gnosticism to be alive and vibrant when materialism begins to falter. Then the trailblazers can lead the people out of darkness and false beliefs, and into the light, the truth."

Sampson nodded. "We can awaken people one at a time. It will be a slow process, but it is achievable."

\* \* \* \* \*

A short time later, Sampson convened the council to solidify the plan of Jesus' life and the events that were to play out. They would utilize several advanced souls who would incarnate at the time of Jesus and shortly after to organize Gnostic groups. The two key figures were Mary Magdalene and John the Baptist. Mary would travel to France and establish what would become the Cathars, the most influential Gnostic group. The Cathars would eventually be murdered by the Catholic Church during the Albigensian Crusade from 1209 to 1229 in Southern France. Their history would mostly be forgotten and lost until the 20th century, when the embers would come back to life.

The followers of John the Baptist would give rise to many secret Gnostic groups. None of them would be clearly linked to John, but his influence would be quite strong. It was these secret groups that kept Gnosticism alive throughout the Middle Ages and the Renaissance. The Knights Templar, Freemasons, and Rosicrucians are good examples of these secretive Gnostic groups. These groups never shared their beliefs with the public for a variety of reasons, but they were able to keep the beliefs alive.

Most of the Gnostics who carried forward the message did so as individuals. These were advanced soul volunteers who were sent to keep the beliefs alive. Many of these people were from India, although there were some from Europe and other parts of the world. The truth was not allowed to die, even though it could not easily be shared with the mainstream populace. It was to be hidden and kept out of sight.

Towards the end of individualism and materialism, many of the early Gnostic writings would come back to life. They would be hidden in caves for more than a thousand years, and then be found when the time was right. These writings would contradict the New Testament in many ways, and reveal Gnostic teachings attributed to Jesus that were not in the New Testament. For instance, there would be a Gospel of Mary based on Mary Magdalene that was clearly Gnostic. There would be many different Gnostic gospels found, such as the Nag Hammadi scrolls. It would be known that these gospels existed at the time the New Testament was written, and were not only systematically rejected, but deemed heretical and destroyed.

People would come to ask the important question: why were these gospels purged if they were clearly written by Jesus' disciples? And why were the Gnostic versions all rejected? Could it have something to do with the fact that the Gnostics were largely non-religious people who sought to have a *direct* relationship with God? For instance, what is the point of having a church or going to church, if you can have this relationship at home? This is the reason why the Cathars never built a church.

# Chapter Two

# THE VOLUNTEERS

Gabe was born on April 2, 1960 in Perth, Australia. This made him an Aries and a Six of Spades.[3] If you added up the digits of his birthday, it came to 22 (4 + 2 + 1 + 9 + 6), which translates to a life path of four. He was a third-level old soul.

Like most of the volunteers, Gabe was considered unusual by those around him. He never felt he fit in with society, and knew at an early age that he was a stranger in a strange land. He knew that his soul existed and was much more than his physical body. He began having out-of-body experiences at seven years of age, as well as communication with his spirit guides.

As an Aries he was an initiator and had a lot of energy. He also was a Libra rising, which inspired him to read incessantly. By the time he was eighteen, he knew more than most college professors. But his knowledge was mostly esoteric in nature. He knew how life worked and its meaning.

As a Six of Spades, his life was fated. It is the perfect card for those with a mission to accomplish. For those with this birth card, all they need do is stay on the path, and life will unfold magically. In fact, those who are a Six of Spades typically are closely connected to their past lives. What they have prepared for is now manifested in this lifetime. Often they have fewer choices and less freedom and are destined to follow the path that was put into motion in a previous life.[4] This was the case with Gabe.

---

3       1 = Ace of Hearts, 13 = King of Hearts, 14 = Ace of Clubs, 26 = King of Clubs, 27 = Ace of Diamonds, 39 = King of Diamonds, 40 = Ace of Spades, 52 = King of Spades. To calculate your card, multiply your month x 2, add the day, then subtract from 55. For instance, my birthday is March 18th. 3 x 2 = 6 + 18 = 24. 55 – 24 = 31. 31 = 5 of Diamonds.

4       Love Cards, Robert Camp, Sourcebooks Inc., 2004, p. 132.

Gabe came into this life with only one objective, and that was to raise the vibration of the planet. In his recent previous lives, he had been doing this as part of a team. They would infiltrate planets that needed to progress, and they would incarnate and help with that progression. In many respects, he was a teacher, a teacher of how to live life in the most harmonious way.

Six of Spades can be very powerful if they align themselves with the higher good. They have so much help from the other side (spiritual dimensions) that nothing can get in their way. However, because of this close connection to the other side, they can be stubborn in fulfilling their mission. This single-mindedness usually creates problems for the Six of Spades when it comes to relationships and romance, as they have a hard time giving up their freedom and can seem obsessed by the desire to accomplish their objectives.[5]

Gabe was indeed a powerful person, and in many respects, he was obsessed by his objectives. His relationships were a disaster and he was currently single. His problem was that his desire for a relationship was not strong enough to overcome his obsession with helping the planet to evolve.

Being a 22/4 lifepath, his goal in life was to use cooperation, responsibility, and teamwork to create a secure and stable foundation.[6] He was here to be part of a team and to work in cooperation in creating a new civilization. When you combine that with a Six of Spades, you are going to get someone who is obsessed with their goal. And then when you combine that with an Aries with Libra rising, you are going to get someone with inexhaustible energy, plus a reading and knowledge fetish.

There are some additional positive characteristics from being a 22/4, and this is where Gabe shined. Remember, he was a third-level old soul and had lived many lives as a spiritual teacher. Those

---

5     Ibid.

6     The Life You Were Born To Live, Dan Millman, H J Kramer, 1993, p. 196.

on a 22/4 lifepath can only achieve their goals using cooperation and teamwork. In other words, he could not use arrogance or pushiness to achieve his goals. He had to be empathetic and understanding, and work in cooperation with others to help the planet raise its vibration.

The 22 is a double 2, which is partnership and relationships. While Gabe had trouble with romantic relationships due to his tendency, as a Six of Spades, toward obsessiveness, he was able to form other types of relationships that helped him accomplish his goal. He became a Life Coach and helped people to improve their lives. Being a 22 was a perfect number for his profession. He could quickly form very good relationships with his clients.

Also, 22s can accomplish anything they set out to do. So when you have someone who is a 22 with a Six of Spades, and is also third-level old soul, you have a dynamo. And that was Gabe. He loved his job and woke up each morning with a smile on his face, ready to go. Every client was different, but they all wanted the same thing: a better life. There was something wrong or lacking in their lives and they couldn't fix it on their own.

Most of Gabe's clients found him from his website, but he also posted flyers around town. He had been doing this for twenty years, so many of his customers were either repeat customers or heard about him from a friend.

＊　＊　＊　＊　＊

On this day, Gabe was coaching someone new. They were going to spend the entire day together. Gabe called this an intensive, which he offered to spiritual students, for those who wanted to get closer to their soul and become more spiritually aware.

They would spend the first two hours at Gabe's house doing a life between life (LBL) regression, and learning how to prepare for each day. Then they would have a sound balancing, followed by a trip to a sacred site near Perth called the Pinnacles.

Gabe sat Juliet in the comfortable leather chair that he used for his life between life (LBL) regressions. This was in one of his three bedrooms, which was specifically used for regressions. The room was full of crystals and new-age paraphernalia, including a Buddha, an ankh symbol, several fairies and angels, a mandala, and pictures of both Jesus and Mary Magdalene. The door was shut and the lights were dimmed, creating a very dark atmosphere. Candles and incense were burning.

Gabe used his standard procedure to regress Juliet. His objective was to connect to her higher self and find out what Juliet was trying to achieve in this lifetime.

"Go to the time of preparation for this lifetime. Go to the time when you are planning for this lifetime and what you are going achieve…. Describe where you are."

Gabe waited.

"I am in a room with one of my guides. This is where we usually meet. I think the room is made out of crystal. It seems like glass, but I know it is stone. I can't see through it, so it must be very thick. There is nothing on the walls and there are no doors, which seems odd. We are alone, but I can sense others who are nearby. They might not be in the next room, but they are not far away.

"My guide is highly evolved and has been helping me to accomplish what I need. He is standing in front of me, wearing his usual white robe. He is telling me that I need to go to Earth to help during the transition. I am going to be a woman who raises two exceptional girls. They will become strong women who help humanity to evolve. It is my responsibility to make sure that I am a good mother and that I sacrifice my needs and my ego in support of my children. He says that my children must be my priority, and that by focusing on raising them, it will bring me closer to God.

"My horoscope, numerology, and energy patterns will all be determined prior to my birth. This will be the same for my two girls. We will be given what we need to accomplish our goals, including experienced spirit guides. We are all old souls and will be Spades for this incarnation. My girls will both be Aquarians only a year apart. I will be a Cancer, born in July, with strong motherly tendencies.

"I am to learn metaphysics and teach it to my children. They in turn will teach it to humanity. It is possible I will be a single mother, because all of my focus will be on my children. They will be all I care about."

The regression lasted about thirty minutes, and Juliet was conscious throughout. She remembered it as if it were a normal experience.

After Gabe ended the regression and brought her consciousness fully back to the room, Juliet was visibly shaken. "Oh my God! That is why I am here today. My little girls are all I care about. I know I need to do something for them. And my marriage has been a shambles for more than a year now. It is on the verge of ending."

Gabe had heard this many times from his clients. "Not all marriages are meant to last a lifetime. It is natural for some relationships to come to an end. Do not feel that it is your fault that it is ending. Recognize that you are right where you need to be, and that your life is perfect. If you can do that, then I can help you to find your way."

Juliet was crying, but she smiled. "Thank you. I would like that outcome."

"Don't thank me. I am just part of the love of the Creator, and so are you. I'm just playing my part."

She smiled.

"Okay," Gabe said. "Let me teach you how to begin each morning, and then we can be off on our adventure."

Gabe handed her his morning routine.

"I do this every morning when I wake up. First, I sing a Lemurian tone,[7] like this one:

'ah...... maw..... naw.............................'

'kah...... maw..... naw.........................'

'maw...... kah...... lo.............................'

"There are twenty-four tones, so I do a different one every day. The tones are good for balancing your energy field and chakras. They are a self healing modality, and are excellent for keeping you healthy. Also, the 'ah' sound is a good method for connecting to the soul first thing in the morning. The 'ah' sound is the sound of love, which is the core of our being. It is like saying, 'good morning soul!'"

Juliet laughed. "That is the sound people make when making love."

Gabe smiled. "And it is the sound they make when they feel love for a child or a pet animal."

"Yeah," Juliet said. "I hear that sound all the time. It so perfectly expresses the emotion of love."

Gabe nodded. "After I finish toning, I take a couple of deep breaths, and I mentally move my energy from my head down into my heart. I visualize this and tell myself to live each day more from my heart than my head. This has a soothing, calming effect, and allows love into my energy field. Why? Because love comes from the heart, and I just opened it up.

"Next, I put my palms face up, feeling energy come into my hands. Then I'll say, 'Be gentle, kind, calm, and compassionate to others.' And I repeat it with deep thought, 'Be gentle, kind, calm, and compassionate to others.' Followed by feelings of unconditional love, which sums up those words. Sometimes if I feel tense, I'll say, 'Calm down, relax' a few times.

---

7     This is tone number nine. http://www.pinealtones.com

"Then I'll put my palms together as if in prayer, and I say, 'Be in integrity, purity, and innocence.' And I repeat it with deep thought, 'Be integrity, purity, and innocence.' Followed by 'Live by my highest moral values,' which sums up those words. Sometimes I will add, 'Watch your thoughts, actions, and behaviors' a few times to drive home the idea of what being spiritual is all about.

"Then I'll interlock my fingers and I say, 'Be example by being grateful, reverent, and humble.' And I repeat it with deep thought 'Be example by being grateful, reverent, and humble.' Followed by 'Be thankful,' which sums up those words. Sometimes I will list the things in my life that I am thankful for and turn it into a prayer.

"The first part of my routine is done, and now I turn to acknowledging the soul. The first part is about putting the ego in its place. It is about marginalizing the ego so that it does not block the soul and how we want to live our lives. Anytime we are stuck or blocked, it is the ego getting in our way. The first part of this morning routine gets the ego out of our way.

"The second part is to acknowledge the soul. Do this by recognizing the core of who you are. I say 'The soul: grounded, centered, connected.' And of course, I repeat it with deep thought: 'The soul: grounded, centered, connected.' I like to visualize each of these words when I say them. For grounding, I visualize a rope around my waist with a weight on the end hanging deep down into the earth. For centering, I visualize that the spiritual planes are both above and below me, and that I am living in the physical world centered between them. For connecting, I visualize myself connected to my spirit guides around the table. I see all of us holding hands with our etheric light bodies.

"The last thing I do is picture myself surrounded in white light, and I say 'I AM,' then I picture my spirit guides seated with me at the table, and I say 'We ARE,' then I picture the planet surrounded in white light, and I say 'God IS.' I repeat this one time and end it with 'Namaste.' Sometimes I press my palms together in the form of a prayer, and then I nod, as a tribute to the Creator.

"I also like to keep a count of how long I have been doing this. The count acknowledges how many days I have been in union with spirit. My number is 787, and tomorrow it will be 788. So when someone asks me, 'What's your number?' I can tell them. I've been doing this routine for almost three years."

Gabe smiled.

Juliet did not return his smile. She was all business now that she knew what she was on this planet to accomplish. "Should I keep count?"

"Absolutely," he replied. "Your number is what will get you through the day. It will keep you innocent, and it will keep you connected to your spirit. After you start doing this each day, you will not want to stop. I have a saying, 'I'm not going back to zero.' Once you begin your spiritual path, you will not want to stop."

Everything that Gabe had told her, he had given to her as a printout. She would have no problem duplicating it.

Gabe smiled. "Okay, let's hit the road."

\* \* \* \* \*

The first stop was Echoes Sound Healing, about fifteen minutes south of downtown Perth. The sound healing sessions at Echoes were held in a teepee, tucked away in an obscure location behind a restaurant. Unless you were looking for it, you wouldn't know it was there.

The teepee had room for only thirteen people, so Gabe had made reservations in advance. The sessions lasted about an hour, and they offered three different types: crystal bowls, gongs, and crystal bowls, or gongs, crystal bowls, and didgeridoo. Gabe preferred the session that included the didgeridoo.

Inside the teepee were makeshift beds that faced the center of the room. There were also pillows and blankets, as well as essential oils. Once the sound therapy began, the lights were lowered, and the room became nearly pitch black.

Gabe and Juliet lay down next to each other on their blankets, with their head facing the center of the room, and their feet facing the wall. They had removed their shoes before entering the teepee. One of the facilitators applied essential oils to their foreheads above their nose, anointing and stimulating the third eye.

First there was an explanation of what was going to be done by the facilitators and what to expect, then the lights were dimmed and the sound therapy began. The combined sound of the gongs, crystal bowls, and didgeridoo was powerful. Everyone in the room was inundated with sound, their bodies literally vibrating. It had the effect of balancing their energy fields.

Gabe had done this dozens of times. He used it for rejuvenation and balancing. He always quieted his mind and meditated during the session, allowing his spirit guides entry into his earthly consciousness. Often during the sessions, he would get a download of information, which he remembered later. For instance, his guides gave him ideas for how to conduct his intensives, how to help some of his clients, and even ideas for his morning routine. This wasn't the only place he got direction from his spirit guides. They were always with him and communicated with him at random times. But the sound chamber seemed to open him up to better listening.

Juliet was a virgin to the sound chamber. At first she thought it was as relaxing and invigorating as sex. "Oh, this feels good," she thought to herself. If she had wanted, she could have focused her thoughts on her body and felt extreme ecstasy. But instead she quieted her mind and began to meditate as she was instructed.

As Juliet's body vibrated from the intense sound, she breathed deeply and felt the invigoration. She kept her mind quiet and allowed the sound to heal her. She knew it was doing something profound to her body. She could feel it. When the gong was played to a crescendo, she thought it was amazing that she had never heard of sound therapy before.

Once the session was over, they exited the teepee and retrieved their shoes. Then they walked toward the car. They both felt as if they had just gotten off a rollercoaster. Their bodies were still winding down from vibrating for about 45 minutes, and they felt somewhat delirious and dizzy.

"That was amazing," Juliet said. "I've never experienced anything like that before."

Gabe smiled. "Sound therapy can heal, rejuvenate and act as a catalyst for accessing the soul. I would recommend that you go back, but next time use it for contacting your soul. This first time it is an initiation and I didn't want to tell you what to do. But next time, try to connect with your soul and spirit guides."

"Sure, I could do that. So, what's next on the agenda?"

"We are going to a sacred site, the Pinnacles," Gabe replied.

"Really? That's a long drive."

"Have you ever been there?" Gabe asked.

Juliet smiled. "Of course! I'm a native of Perth."

"Did you know it was a sacred site?"

Juliet slowly shook her head back and forth. "No."

"Today we will approach it from reverence and respect. These stones were revered by ancient civilizations. It is a very special place."

"I can do that," Juliet said.

*　*　*　*　*

Two hours later, they arrived at Nambung National Park, home to the limestone rock formations known as the Pinnacles. Gabe had packed a lunch, and they would have a picnic after viewing many of the stones. As usual, there was no line at the entrance. Gabe paid the entrance fee and drove to his favorite spot, where they parked and got out. The sun was shining brightly, and the blue sky was exhilarating. Very few people were to be seen. The Pinnacles was a long drive from Perth, and there wasn't much traffic on the road. Western Australia was largely uninhabited. The locals normally drove south because there wasn't much to the north or east, where the Pinnacles were located. On busy weekends there could be 250 visitors at one time at the Pinnacles, but on weekdays there were less than half that many.

They got out and began walking among the beautiful large stones. It was eerie and stunning to behold: a desert landscape with stone pillars jutting out of the sand. Visitors were not prohibited from walking anywhere in the park. There were really only two rules: drive slowly and do not climb on the rocks. Both of which were to protect the visitors from hurting themselves and to preserve these natural monoliths.

What amazed Gabe was that these beautiful stones had not been defaced in any way. There was not a single instance of graffiti. Somehow people knew this place was too sacred to deface. Some of the stones were over ten feet tall. The park was only about ten square miles in size, and there were more than a thousand stones. You could walk the entire park in a single day.

Gabe and Juliet started heading towards a cluster of pinnacles. Gabe could instantly feel the difference in the energy. The sun was up, and they could feel the warmth as they walked towards the cluster of huge rocks. Gabe could feel a certain excitement rising within him. He could hear messages in his head that the ancestors of this land were saying 'welcome back' and were pleased to feel his presence. Gabe stood still for a moment and spread his arms wide apart and then brought his palms together in front of his chest as an acknowledgment of thank you to the ancestors.

Gabe had been to the Pinnacles several times in the past and each time was a different experience for him. He was excited and intuitively knew that the energy here would somehow help Juliet to awaken a part of her that was ready to be awakened. Juliet was observing Gabe, curious and wanting to understand what Gabe was doing.

As they came closer to the cluster of huge rocks, one particular stone structure stood out, and Gabe intuitively walked up to it. He could feel the energy and see the image of an ancestor that was so clear in the stone. He tuned in to that energy and got a sense that this was one of the spots that they were meant to visit.

"Feel the reverence for nature," Gabe said. "Go and hug one of the rocks that you feel drawn towards."

Juliet smiled and walked to the nearest rock and hugged it, keeping her her eyes closed.

As she hugged the rock, Gabe stood by her side. "You know, it's as alive as we are. Can you feel your connection to it? Feel its age. Feel the ancients who were here before. Feel your connection to the past."

Tears appeared on Juliet's face. "Oh, this is emotional. These stones are God's footprints, aren't they?"

Gabe nodded. "They are our footprints, too. They are our reminders that not only are the stones sacred, but so are we."

"Now I see why you brought me here. You want me to feel reverence for life, all life."

Gabe nodded. "Reverence, humbleness, gratefulness, humility, and gratitude. They are important concepts that we need to live by, if we want to experience peace, harmony, and completeness."

Juliet smiled. "Oh, I love that word. I want completeness. Can you teach me how to get it?"

"I can show you how, but you have to do the work."

"I have to recite your list every morning?"

Gabe laughed. "For starters, yes. But that is the easy part."

"I'll do what is necessary for my daughters."

Gabe looked into Juliet's eyes. "Women are so strong. I'm in awe of your strength."

Juliet laughed.

"Okay," Gabe said, "let's go find a place for our picnic. We can talk more about your daughters."

They both smiled.

They walked among the large stones on their way back to the car, feeling the majesty and sacredness of the place. Everywhere they looked they could see the amazing stone spires sticking out of the ground. How the stones got here was a mystery. It looked like a desert of sand mixed with these majestic stones. Clearly it was made by nature, but how? Perhaps it would remain one of nature's mysteries.

Gabe drove Juliet to the other side of the park where it tended to be quiet and barren of people. They got out of the car and walked toward the center of the park. He knew an area that was likely to be empty. Juliet carried a blanket, and Gabe the ice chest.

After walking for about five minutes, Gabe found what he was looking for. He put down the ice chest in the shade of a big rock. "This is a good spot. Let me help you with the blanket."

They each took an end of the blanket and sat it down in the shade. There were large and small stones in every direction, along with the ubiquitous dark brown sand. Gabe opened the ice chest and produced two bottles of water, a container of whole strawberries that were cleaned with the tops removed, a container of sliced pineapple, two whole Gala apples, a bag of raw almonds, two fresh baguettes, brie cheese, and a knife. Before he packed the lunch, Gabe had asked Juliet if this menu would be satisfactory.

Gabe sliced a baguette and spread brie on the bread. He handed Juliet the knife, baguette, and cheese. "Here you go. Help yourself."

It was a warm day, and they were both wearing shorts. Without the shade, it would have been uncomfortable. For a while, they were quiet as they ate their lunch and took in their surroundings.

"How old are your daughters?" Gabe asked.

"Four and three."

"You have some time then to do your spiritual work before they require guidance."

Juliet became intrigued and stared at Gabe. "What kind of guidance?"

"We have just begun a transition into a new civilization. The world that your daughters are going to grow up in is going be a different place than what we experienced."

"How so?" she asked.

"The energy grid on the planet is changing. Those who are aware of this change will have a much easier transition. Those who are stuck in the past will have a difficult time adapting. In fact, many will perish, because their energy field will not be compatible with the new crystalline grid."

Gabe paused. He could see in Juliet's eyes that she had not been exposed to this knowledge.

"People today are evolving spiritually at a very rapid pace. This evolution is occurring because the energy grid of the planet is changing, although you could also say the reverse is true, that the energy grid of the planet is changing because people are evolving. Either way, the crystalline energy grid of the planet is changing. This grid impacts our own personal energy fields to such an extent that it literally impacts and can change our DNA."

Juliet reached for a strawberry, but was listening attentively.

"Right now, all over the planet, people's DNA is changing, and for the better. We are becoming more god-like and more loving. Many people are becoming more psychic, with abilities that in the past were rare.

"These changes are not happening to everyone, but only to those who are spiritually aware and more advanced. Thus, many are being left behind because of the spiritual changes that are taking place. What is happening today is a spiritual renaissance, and this spiritual change is impacting everything. This is why the global economies and social systems are breaking down. Those who associate closely with mainstream culture are seeing their lives become stressful and degenerative. Their very way of life is falling apart.

"What we are experiencing today as a civilization are two different groups having nearly opposite experiences. One group is having a spiritual awakening, while the other is experiencing a societal collapse. Soon everyone is going to recognize what this change is all about, and it is going to be shocking to many."

Juliet looked stunned. "I've never thought of it like that, but it makes perfect sense. Society is clearly breaking down, and something has to save it or rescue it. I would never have guessed that it would be a crystalline energy grid, and that this grid would impact both our DNA and spirituality."

Gabe smiled. "I've been reading about this DNA change for years, and now it is happening. Scientists are already finding it in children. There are children being born who are immune to certain diseases, such as AIDS, and this is related to their DNA differences. They are also finding significant DNA differences that they have never seen before in humans. But it is not just children; our DNA is also changing.

"As more and more people become spiritually aware, it impacts the crystalline grid. Then the crystalline grid impacts us. It's a positive reinforcing loop. And, it appears to be growing exponentially. This spiritual awakening that is happening today is going to literally transform humanity into a loving, peaceful society. But more than that, it's going to change everything: our culture, our economics, our social systems, everything. By 2050, we won't recognize society as it exists today."

Juliet had an epiphany. "Does this mean we are building and creating a new society today? That we are the builders? I think so. We are living at the dawning of a new civilization!"

Gabe smiled. "That is what your daughters are here for. They came to build a new society. It's not just them. There are millions of advanced souls who are here today to build this new civilization. It will not be easy, because the vast majority of people are not spiritually aware and do not understand where society is heading. The small minority of advanced souls has to show the way, but also do it in a manner that is accepted by less evolved souls."

"You mean they have to do it subtly?"

Gabe nodded. "Healthy lifestyles, holistic healing, high nutrition diets, use of alternative energy, environmental stewardship, permaculture farming, peaceful coexistence, spiritual awareness, et cetera. These are the new modes of living that we will follow. The evolved souls will show the way in these areas, and then eventually, they will be accepted by everyone.

"The first place it will have a major impact is health and holistic healing. The evolved souls have been using holistic and natural healing methods for decades. These modalities are going to become very effective as the crystalline grid changes. Hospitals and drugs, for the most part, will no longer be necessary. Once people find alternative healing modalities that work, they will stop using pharmaceutical drugs.

"Then, in tandem with new healing modalities, people will start putting healthy food into their bodies. Then once they begin to respect their bodies, they will begin to respect other people and nature. As I like to say, 'It's a slippery slope.' Once you change one thing in your life for the better, the rest of your life begins to change for the better."

Juliet looked stunned. "I think I'm having an OMG moment. I think I get it. The world is having a spiritual awakening. However, only a small minority knows about it. This small minority has to change the world, but in a very slow, subtle manner. They have to awaken the rest of humanity one soul at a time."

Gabe smiled and nodded. "That's it. However, the outcome has been ordained. We will succeed. This planet will soon have a highly evolved civilization. Peace on earth is coming. In our lifetime, we will see that the tipping point has been crossed."

"What do you mean?" Juliet asked.

"It will take about four generations to complete, but during our lifetime, we will see that the outcome is ordained and is coming. We will witness humanity evolving to reach a critical mass whereby change is palpable. When this happens, we will know humanity has crossed a threshold and is evolving toward something beautiful. Peace and love will become palpable. There will be widespread recognition that we made it. That we are going to succeed in creating peace on earth. But there will be work to do, and it will take some time."

"But what if I neglect my role and my daughters become delinquents?"

Gabe laughed. "There is too much interaction from the other side. Why do you think we are together today? Do you think it was random or an accident? No. You were led to me by your spirit guides or higher self. A voice in your head said to call me. Then once you got in my presence, your guides told you to listen carefully. Now you are ready to teach your daughters about what is happening in the world today.

"This is how it works. The other side is constantly intervening in our lives. Even if you tried to mislead your daughters, they have spirit guides too. They will likely accomplish their goals even if you don't help them. But if you do help them, then they can accomplish more."

Juliet had that stunned look again. "Wow, the world is a very complex place."

"You have no idea. For every single human, there are many on the other side who are helping them. And their lives blend together with others in a complex web of interaction. And every soul that is incarnate on this planet has personal goals and missions that they are trying to accomplish. Some of these goals have nothing to do with this planet and are simply part of their soul growth.

"So while this planet is trying to evolve and impact the entire universe, so is each individual soul. There are layers and layers of purposes and plans for individual souls, planets, civilizations, and even universes. The web of complexity is beyond our understanding."

Juliet had a piece of pineapple. "Now I see why you do your morning routine, and why it is so important. Life is so much bigger than we imagine. We think it is just this lifetime, but that is the illusion, isn't it? Somehow we have to see through the illusion and understand the truth of life."

Gabe nodded. "Exactly. We have to look beyond this illusion and see the bigger picture."

Juliet had a drink from her water bottle. "I can do that."

Gabe smiled. "I think your spirit guides are happy today. You are on the right path now. All you need to do now is follow it."

Gabe paused and looked seriously and Juliet. "It's time for the red pill."

"What?" Julie asked.

"Do you know who you are? Who we are?"

"Is this a riddle, or a trick question?" Juliet asked, surprised.

"No, it was a serious question. Let me rephrase. Do you think it's possible that there is only one consciousness, which we all share?"

Juliet thought about the question, but did not reply.

"Let me answer it for you," Gabe replied. "The answer is yes. There is only one consciousness. It is the consciousness of the Creator. Subsequently, you and I are part of that consciousness. In effect, there is no separation between anything. Separation is a lie. The only thing that exists is the Creator.

"This is the objective truth, although science won't prove it for about three more decades. However, many in society will know this truth long before that time. This is the truth that brings peace and harmony to humankind. This is the truth that sets us free."

Juliet looked stunned. "So, then I am God and you are God?"

Gabe nodded. "The only blasphemy is the denial of the divine. When you look at something outside of yourself and don't see the divine, you are in denial."

"What about evil?" Juliet asked.

"Let me say this, and then you can rephrase your question. Since everthing is the Creator, everything is perfection because the Creator only knows perfection. Is it really evil, if it is perfection? And let me add that since we are part of the Creator, we are eternal."

Juliet paused to think. "You are implying that we expose ourselves to evil for a reason? What is that reason?"

Gabe grinned, waiting for Juliet to figure it out.

"To evolve?"

Gabe nodded. "Yes. To know hate, you must experience it. To know cruelty, you must experience it. The Creator desires to experience everything. Note that most planets are loving and harmonious. The degree of darkness on this planet is rare in the cosmos Earth school is highly prized for its diversity. We are very fortunate to get to experience this opportunity."

Julie looked in awe. "So, the truth is that we are God! That's stunning. And humanity is going to learn this truth?"

Gabe nodded. "It begins very soon. The truth is going to be released. Well, actually, it is being released, but the pace will pick up soon, and all of humanity will know. Most will initially reject it, but the truth will win."

"That's how we create peace," Juliet said softly.

Gabe nodded. "If we recognize that we are one, war will stop, inhumanity will stop. Love and harmony will arise. We get to be the generation that starts the wave of awareness. Actually, we get to the generation that is told the truth. It will take four generations for the truth to be completely accepted by humanity."

"That's a lot of information to process," Julie said, stunned.

"Sorry for the red pill. But don't worry, your head won't explode. You can now have hope for the future. This is a good thing."

"I know, but it's also hard to wrap my head around. I'm God?" Juliet said incredulously.

Gabe smiled. "You can handle the truth. Your daughters are going to love it."

# Chapter Three

# THE OTHER SIDE

Sampson was conflicted. He had been overseeing project Earth Awaken, and something was bothering him. Thousands of the volunteers had gone astray from their goals. It didn't matter how skilled their spirit guides were, if the volunteers didn't want to listen, then the guides could not help. He had been working with many spirit guides from the 7th dimension, and the reports he was receiving were troubling. He decided to meet with Mestos to discuss the problem.

They were in a room with a large screen similar to a small movie theatre. On this level of existence, there was no physical matter, but it looked real nonetheless. Sampson projected the life of Lisa on the screen. There was no projector and the screen came to life as if by magic. There on the screen was Lisa living her life in San Diego.

She was sitting on her sofa eating chips and watching television, and thinking about her boyfriend. Not only could they see her on the screen, but they could hear her thoughts telepathically. In addition, they could feel her emotions. Even more than that, they could sense her energy field and any health-related issues.

Mestos looked at the screen with the calm demeanor typical of those from the 9th dimension. "Sampson, why are you showing me this?"

"I want to show you what we are seeing. She is an example of thousands of volunteers who have strayed from their mission."

Mestos nodded. "Okay, tell me about her."

"She is a third-level old soul. A Two of Spades, Capricorn with Cancer rising. Born on January 12, 1972, making her a 29/11, with a 2 lifepath. A massage therapist in San Diego. In her most recent lives, she has been a systems breaker, volunteering to help planets evolve by changing their belief systems. She usually likes the tough jobs, but Earth has stymied her. If Lisa is failing, you can imagine how many other volunteers are having difficulty."

Mestos contemplated. "We can't let this happen. Our volunteers are too important for this project. Let's take a look at her life and see what we can do for her."

Sampson looked at Mestos. "You mean intervene?"

Mestos nodded. "Yes, let's get her back on her path."

"Is that the right thing to do, Mestos? Aren't we going to interfere with her free will?"

"Sampson, her spirit guides do this all the time. They are constantly guiding her."

"But Mestos, that is different. They are trained to work *with* her free will, and not circumvent it."

"Sampson, for this project, it is okay if we help our volunteers to achieve their goals. They came to save the planet, and it is our job to help them do that. We cannot stand by and watch them fail."

Sampson nodded. "Okay. This is your project, and I will let you make that decision. What's next?"

Mestos grinned. "Let's look at her life. I can see that she is not focused on her mission. She seems to be escaping through food and entertainment, and her health is failing. What year is it?"

"It's 2013," Sampson replied.

"Let's rewind to when she is working."

Magically, the screen immediately displayed Lisa working on one of her clients, giving a massage. Mestos and Sampson studied her thoughts, feelings and energy field. It was not good. She was going through the motions, but her mind was not on her job. Instead, she was thinking about food and her boyfriend, as well as having negative thoughts about her body and health.

"Emotionally, she is not satisfied," Mestos said. "She is spending too much time identifying with her ego." Mestos paused. "Show me a recent experience she had with her boyfriend."

Immediately the screen changed and showed Lisa together with her boyfriend. It only took a few seconds, but it was apparent that her boyfriend did not love her and was only dating her for sex.

"There is part of your problem," Mestos replied. "She is a 2 lifepath and doesn't want to be alone. She needs to be in love with a reliable companion to accomplish her mission. Tell her spirit guides to get a much more suitable partner to cross her path, a man that she finds attractive and will feel an instant connection. Tell them to do whatever they can to help her find her chosen path, which is helping humanity evolve. Let her spirit guides know that this is a special situation and comes from project Earth Awaken."

"Okay, I'll inform her guides, and we'll try it," Sampson said.

\* \* \* \* \*

Lisa's spirit guides were informed to help Lisa accomplish her mission. They were to remove anything that was blocking her way. An additional spirit guide was added to give a new perspective. This gave her three spirit guides.

The first thing the guides did was to break up Lisa's romantic relationship. This was easy to accomplish. First, they began giving her suggestions that her boyfriend did not love her and was only after sex. Then they interacted with his spirit guides, who were very accommodating, based on Lisa's mission as a volunteer, to get him to show his true colors. It only took two weeks before Lisa broke up with him.

Next, they had a friend of hers invite Lisa to a meetup group that was focused on ascension. She began meeting each week with the group and reading material regarding ascension. This group had weekend meetings where they had potlucks. Most of the members were old souls and tended to be either vegetarian or vegan. After a few weeks, Lisa's diet began to improve, and she started losing weight.

One day at one of the meetings, a guy attended who got Lisa's eye. It was no accident that he appeared. His spirit guides had him search the meetup groups in San Diego, and they nudged him to attend. They knew he was compatible with Lisa. And when he walked in the room, Lisa's spirit guides practically yelled into her ear, "Look over there!"

When they met for the first time, Lisa flirted with him and asked him to come back the following week. When he did come back, Lisa made sure to wear a form-fitting blouse to get his attention. It worked. Of course it worked; his guides had been informed that this relationship was good for both of them. When the spirit guides of both genders are working in concert, it is almost impossible to fail. Why do you think so many people get into relationships and marriages? If it wasn't for help from the other side, most relationships would never happen.

It wasn't long before Lisa was in love, and her thoughts were back to more pressing concerns of helping humanity. Her depth of compassion and strong will made her a natural volunteer. Being a Capricorn and a Cancer rising, she was a very strong motherly type. Humanity was her family, and she was going to look out for their well-being. Her 2 lifepath could now be realized. She could have relationships with many friends and acquaintances and help show them the way. Now her massages were filled with love, and she injected her love into her clients. More than that, she was literally healing many of her clients with her healing hands. Many of them came back every month because they knew it was more than just a massage.

\* \* \* \* \*

Sampson was jubilant. He met again with Mestos to tell him of the progress they were making. To meet with Mestos, all he had to do was think of him, and Mestos would appear. On this level of existence, they could literally manifest multiple instances of their identity. The soul was capable of splitting into distinct pieces of consciousness and existing at multiple locations simultaneously. In fact, the soul could exist on both the spiritual dimensions and physical dimensions simultaneously in multiple bodies. There were truly no limitations.

"It worked, Mestos. Lisa is accomplishing her mission. Your advice of giving her what she needed worked."

Mestos nodded. He was not surprised. He had checked several of her possible timelines and knew she would likely find the correct path.

"Mestos, I am going to work with the spirit guides to help many of the other volunteers who have gone astray. There are tens of thousands we can help, maybe even hundreds of thousands."

"Sampson, that is an ideal plan. They are getting very close now for when the changes to intensify. We have already succeeded in saving the planet from destruction. Now I want to ensure that a New Earth is manifested and millions of souls ascend."

"Mestos, I will do everything I can to make it happen. I think your plan is going to work. I have confidence that a New Earth will manifest and there will be a mass ascension. All of the souls who ascend will get to experience something quite wondrous and profound. I myself would not mind such an experience."

Sampson smiled. "Nor I. I think this is why there are so many extraterrestrials watching this event and are planning to become involved once the changes intensify. Everyone in the universe wants this to be successful."

"Indeed," Mestos replied, "it is a huge event, and we are near culmination. Every soul that awakens now increases the strength of the crystalline grid. We are getting close to the change point where the grid literally pushes many souls into a new dimension, to the New Earth."

Sampson nodded. "As the crystalline grid strengthens, it transforms their DNA. Thus, this transformation leads to a natural ascension process."

Mestos smiled. "Yes, their DNA is changing as we speak. As the grid changes, it is changing their DNA. This makes ascension inevitable for those souls who are ready."

"Mestos, I know that you like to analyze future timelines for possible outcomes. What timeline is now the most probable for the first wave of ascension?"

"There are currently three that are most probable. I don't know which of the three Earth's mass consciousness will choose. Why don't we look at them?"

In that instant, a large screen appeared in front of them, and they could see images of the future. The images were no different from a real-life video. In fact, these were the actual images that could easily manifest in the future.

Life is playback. Nothing happens that isn't already the imagination of God. All outcomes are already known by the Creator. This is why there are no accidents. Before a soul is incarnated, it can view its future lifetime, and it can look at God's imagination. It can't view it frame by frame because there are too many possibilities. But it can view many scenes which could occur and many timelines that are possible. It can view the worst (negative) outcomes and the best (positive).

Free will does exist, but it is complex with many paradoxes. We do have free will to make choices on how we are going to evolve. However, if these choices impact others, then our free will can be limited. Everything has to coexist in a huge interplay of experiences. Everyone has their own goals, which are chosen prior to their incarnation, and can't be impeded by others. As you can imagine, if everyone had complete free will, then life would be a mess, and few would accomplish their life goals.

The scene that played before them showed mass chaos. Police officers were using their authority and power to maintain control of what appeared to be a large crowd of protestors. It was ugly, with armed men in black uniforms arresting random people. The scene took place in a large city where thousands were protesting and getting arrested. There were tear gas fumes and fires throughout the downtown area.

"The changes begin to manifest after 2012," Mestos began, "increasing in intensity around 2020. I have been looking at the timelines from that period until 2030. What you are seeing is an outcome I would not prefer. If you can awaken more souls, there is a chance this won't happen. But time is running out."

After a few seconds, the large screen showed another location. There were scenes of long lines where people were waiting. They waited for food, employment, government relief, banks, even healthcare. There seemed to be lines everywhere. It was a chaotic time, and people were traumatized.

The next scene of another probable future was better, with people smiling and cooperating. It was clear that society had fallen on hard times, but it was happening in a more orderly manner where people accepted the outcome and were trying to create positive change. The government and the economy had become ineffective in turning things around, and people were learning how to work together to solve problems. An amazing amount of love and interconnectedness had invigorated people. There was a sense that they would survive.

"Is this the New Earth?" Sampson asked.

"No, but they are getting closer to the time of ascension. This is a small town in Northern California, but this same reaction could occur over most of the world after soceity begins to break down."

The screen disappeared. "I don't need to show you any more scenes. The difference in the timelines is the degree of spiritual awakening that occurs prior to society breaking down. The more awakening that occurs, the less chaos and trauma. The good news is that the worst outcome is short-lived and lasts only about five years."

"Mestos, what outcome is the most likely to transpire?"

"It's too soon to say. The mass consciousness on Earth has not yet decided how much chaos and trauma to experience. I think it is inevitable that we will see a large degree of chaos, especially in the big cities. But I am hopeful that humans will respond to these traumatic changes by working closely together."

"Do you think the extraterrestrials will provide a calming effect?" Sampson asked.

Mestos nodded. "That's part of the plan. They will land shortly after the changes intensify and make their presence known to the entire planet. The first wave of ascension will come shortly thereafter. So we need to ensure that as many souls as possible are ready for ascension during that timeframe."

"Okay," Sampson concluded, "I will work with the spirit guides to awaken as many souls as possible to populate the New Earth. What about the Old Earth?"

"It will steadily depopulate over the next six thousand years. There will be only plants and animals in six thousand years. Humans will all move to the New Earth, which will be a fifth-dimensional planet."

"And the Old Earth will be third, fourth, and fifth dimensional until it is depopulated?"

Mestos nodded, and his spirit body disappeared.

*  *  *  *  *

Sampson gathered a council from the 7th dimension to discuss new plans for project Earth Awaken. Each member of the council was in charge of thousands of spirit guides. They weren't really "in charge," but acted as highly respected advisors. This particular council specialized in the volunteers assigned to Earth.

The council formed a semicircle of twenty-three souls. Sampson created the meeting to show the council a few examples of volunteers who needed help. He could manifest a meeting in a few minutes. It didn't take long. On the 7th and 9th dimensions, souls could manifest anything they desired with their divine consciousness. They were literally god-like.

If a soul was called to a meeting, they would simply send a portion of their soul consciousness to the meeting. They would appear to be fully present, and you could not tell that they were not. To give an analogy, it was similar to the 1996 movie Multiplicity, in which the main character, played by Michael Keaton, clones himself to make life easier. On the spiritual dimensions, the higher self of the soul kept everything organized. All of the experiences of the soul ended up with the higher self, which was an amalgamation of these experiences.

The souls on the council were mostly semi-transparent, and if you looked closely, they appeared as wispy manifestations of male or female entities. Most were dressed in robes, although some appeared as energetic light beings without clothing. Some of them looked human, while others looked quite non-human. It didn't matter; they were just manifestations.

Sampson sat in the center of the semicircle with eleven members on either side. They were each seated in a chair behind a large semicircular table. There was no need for chairs or a table, but Sampson preferred a more formal design to create reverence.

He began the meeting by showing scenes of Lisa's life before and after the intervention of her spirit guides. Then he began to speak telepathically to the council.

"Mestos has recommended that we help the volunteers achieve their objectives and that we focus on those who have gone astray. This is an example of how we succeeded in changing one volunteer's life. Lisa was floundering, and her spirit guides, out of respect to her free will, were allowing her to find her own way. Had we not intervened, the chances were that she would not have been able to impact the world with her gifts. And without her impact, many souls would not awaken.

"There are many like Lisa whom we can help. Thousands of volunteers have lost their way and are not accomplishing their mission. The more volunteers we can help, the more impact they can have on humanity. Those volunteers who are floundering as Lisa was should be given guidance to find their chosen path."

Sampson paused for a response.

"Is this in conformance with the laws of free will?" one of the council members asked.

There were a few murmurs, as this was the question on many of these souls' minds.

"This is a special situation," Sampson replied. "These are volunteers whom we sent in to accomplish a mission. Not just any mission, but an important mission to save a civilization that could impact the entire universe. That is their objective, and it is perfectly allowable for us to help them achieve this objective.

"Under normal circumstances, we allow incarnated souls the free will to grow and evolve. But free will is always limited by the will of the Creator. For instance, when a soul incarnates, they do not have the free will to blow up a planet. Nor do they have the free will to kill another soul unless there is a soul agreement. There are many limitations to free will, and many ways to impact it.

"For the purposes of project Earth Awaken, we have been given the latitude to decide whether we want to impact a volunteer's free will. Mestos has chosen to help the volunteers achieve their objectives. I have no problem with his decision."

There was silence as the council contemplated.

"This is Mestos' project," replied one of the souls on the council. "If he thinks it is appropriate to help the volunteers, then that is fine with me."

The other souls nodded in concurrence.

"Let's not forget," Sampson said, "that many of the volunteers are already getting significant guidance on a daily basis. They are being led to follow their lifepath. The only difference is that these souls have already found their path. Now that they have found it, their guides are doing everything they can to help them stay on it. This new initiative is not that much different. All we are doing to is helping them to find their lifepath in order to achieve their objective.

"Free will is really about soul growth. The Creator gave us free will so that we can develop our soul in our own preferred way. We need to have the freedom to choose our own experiences in order to awaken. But that process is not relevant to the volunteers. They are on a mission to help humanity, and not as an incarnation to develop their soul."

Sampson paused and filled the screen in front of the room with a video of someone living their life on Earth. It was a scene from someone's life in the early 21st century.

"When we began this meeting, I showed you scenes from Lisa's life before we intervened and after. I would like to show you one more example, and then you can convey what is needed to the spirit guides of the volunteers who have gone astray.

"This is Charles." The screen came to life and showed a man sitting outside on his porch reading. "He is thirty-eight. A fifth-level old soul. A Libra with a fine soul and a wonderful heart.

He is a systems breaker and has volunteered numerous times to help planets evolve. This time is he is stuck. He has a trust fund and spends his time at home reading. We need to get him out of the house and into contact with others, but there is a problem. He has created a self-induced fear of the outside world. They call it agoraphobia on Earth. He has been using it as an excuse to stay at home, but this only makes the condition worse.

"Charles is an expert on crystals and their healing properties, which is knowledge he brought with him from past lives. He knows that he should be writing a book about crystals and their properties in order to help others. But his agoraphobia is preventing him from sharing his knowledge.

"There are many gifted volunteers like Charles who are stuck, and are not accomplishing their mission and lifepath. For Charles, all we need to do is study him closely and determine the best method of helping him. In his case, the key is his love of women, especially women with attractive bodies. Find a woman who is interested in crystals and get them to meet. Then help them form a strong romantic relationship. She will be able to cure his agoraphobia and inspire him to write a book and lecture, and to bring out the potential that he holds."

Sampson paused and waited for a response.

"And if the woman fails to cure his agoraphobia?" a council member asked. "We find another method?"

Sampson nodded. "Exactly. Whatever it takes. Find out what these volunteers need, and help them to accomplish their objectives."

"I think this is brilliant," said one of the souls on the council. "You are increasing the rate of how many souls awaken. This will have a significant impact on the crystalline grid and the positive reinforcement loop. As more people awaken, it will make it easier for others to awaken. By focusing on the most evolved souls – the volunteers – you can awaken them much more quickly. They are literally hours, weeks, or months away from an epiphany of knowing."

Sampson smiled. "Mestos will be happy to hear that everyone agrees with his plan. The timelines all support a quickening from the time we implement this new change until the first mass ascension. Once tens of thousands of volunteers are given help, it creates a wave of awakening that sweeps across the planet. It is there to be seen in the Akashic records of the future. There is a clear demarcation when the plan is put into effect."

"What year?" someone asked.

"The first wave of awakening will begin in the late 20th century and early 21st century and will be confined mostly to the volunteers. But they begin to set the seeds in the minds of others. By the year 2025, the awakening will be growing dramatically, although not yet acknowledged by the mainstream. That won't happen until around 2030."

"When will the DNA changes begin?" another council member asked.

"The DNA changes will be very subtle at first," Sampson replied. "Very few will even notice until around 2025. As the crystalline grid strengthens, the planet will steadily get closer and closer to ascension. The first wave of ascension will happen sometime between 2030 and 2050. At this time, there are several different timelines that can be chosen by the mass consciousness."

"Then this meeting is the key?" a council member asked. "We are the ones who put it into motion what creates these timelines?"

Sampson nodded. "Indeed. Does everyone feel puffy?"

The council members laughed. After all, there was plenty of laughter on the higher dimensions, albeit telepathic laughter.

"One last question, Sampson. Is there anything we should be concerned about? Is your plan foolproof?"

There was silence as everyone waited for Sampson to reply.

"I, too, have had your doubts. After all, this has never been achieved before on a planetary level. I have seen the future timelines, and Mestos assures me we will succeed. However, Earth is a planet of free will, and I cannot guarantee certainty. I myself no longer have any doubts. I ask all of you to relinquish your doubts as well. I ask you to have faith."

Sampson waited to see if there were any skeptics. He could feel their energy, and he did not sense one. On this plane of existence, it was impossible to hide one's true feelings.

Sampson nodded, and then the rest of the council nodded in agreement.

"Please take these new plans back to the 7th dimension and share them with the spirit guides. We want to help as many volunteers as possible. I thank you for coming."

Sampson nodded and then slowly disappeared, along with the table and chairs.

# Chapter Four

# THE SPIRIT GUIDES

After Sampson met with the council, there was a frenzy of activity on the 7th dimension. Each of the twenty-two council members met with thousands of spirit guides. Because they communicated telepathically, they could literally hold meetings with thousands of souls at one time.

At these meetings, it was explained that all volunteers on Earth who were not achieving their mission were to be given whatever they needed to find their path. There were no limitations on what could be done as long as the result was to obtain something that was already planned. The guides were told to use their creativity to help these souls find their path. This was the path that the volunteers had already chosen to follow before they incarnated.

The spirit guides were excited to hear this news and proceeded to help the volunteers in any way they could. Some of the spirit guides worked with many incarnated souls at one time. For instance, Tibus was too talented to work with only one soul. Instead, he would monitor thousands of souls on Earth and then interact with their spirit guides. In many respects, he was a mentor for other spirit guides. After project Earth Awaken began, he was especially drawn to the volunteers. Now with this new initiative, his talents were especially useful.

Most of the spirit guides resided in the 5th and 6th dimensions. When beings evolved to the 7th dimension, their skills and awareness progressed past the point of focusing on helping a single soul. Tibus resided on the 7th dimension. However, he enjoyed being a spirit guide to such an extent that he had not moved on to new projects.

He was an ascended master, as were all souls on the 7th dimension or higher. His level of spiritual awareness and spiritual knowledge was vast. He had incarnated over 1,000 lifetimes, including a few on Earth in Lemuria and Atlantis.

Tibus was such a gifted teacher that he always had a few protégés who tended to follow him around. He did not mind, and welcomed any soul who came his way. On this day, he held a small meeting with his group.

Tibus put out a mental call to those who were with him to gather round. Nearly a dozen souls immediately appeared in his company. He liked blue sky, bright green grass, beautiful trees and water, such as ponds, lakes, rivers, and streams. These he manifested as a backdrop. He also included several different animals, including many hummingbirds and butterflies. This was all manifested by him and was completely illusion, as was everything on this dimension.

The dozen souls who gathered with Tibus all wore white robes with gold belts. Their robes and belts were not quite identical, but very similar. They manifested their attire to emulate what Tibus wore. If you asked one of the souls why they did not choose to wear something different, they would not have given a reason that made any sense. They probably would have said something like, "There is no need to wear anything different," or perhaps, "This makes Tibus comfortable." Of course, Tibus could care less what they wore.

They all sat on a large blanket on the grass. The weather was perfect, although they could feel nothing. Tibus was on one end of the blanket and his protégés on the other. They were already informed about the new initiative for the volunteers on Earth.

Tibus addressed his students. "Each of you are monitoring several of the project Earth Awaken volunteers. I want you to pair up with your usual partners and do an overview of each of your volunteers who are having problems. I want you to work together as a team and come up with ideas for actions that you can implement quickly. Once you have an idea that can help one of your volunteers to achieve their objective, I want you to implement it. Interact with their primary spirit guides. They should be accommodating if you explain why you are doing it. Once you are done, move on to the next of your volunteers. After you finish with your volunteers, come and see me, and I will find more for you to help.

"For those of you who do not have a partner, you can monitor me and learn some of my methods. It would be a good learning experience for some of you. I have been monitoring many of the volunteers, and there are many that I intend to help. With our combined efforts, I think we can have an impact on Earth's impending ascension. As you all know, it is important that Earth succeed. I lived a lifetime in Lemuria prior to the fall, and one in Atlantis shortly after the fall. I feel a very close affinity to this project and its success. It is my intention to devote all of my energy to this project. I hope all of you will join me."

All of the souls nodded. With their nods, Tibus could read their energy and know their responses. He could even tell which of the souls had more passion for the project than the others. On this level, nothing could be hidden. Everything was an open book.

"Unless anyone has any questions, let's get to work."

All of the souls had already been briefed on the new mandate to help the volunteers on Earth to achieve their objectives. They were waiting for Tibus' lead on how they should proceed. Most of them understood what was needed and did not have any questions.

"Tibus, what year or period should we focus on?" one of the souls asked.

"The transition period begins to intensify around 2016," he replied. "I would try to have the volunteers on their correct path before or shortly after that period. Try not to go much later than 2020. I would advise to begin around 2010, and then continue helping them until 2020 if necessary. If they are not on their chosen path by 2020, then move on to another volunteer. The period from 2010 to 2020 is the critical period, leading up to when the changes intensify. By 2020, the planet should begin to change, and we want to make sure they are ready for that period so that they can help the planet awaken."

Tibus paused to see if that was a sufficient answer. He could tell by reading their energy that it was. He arose from the blanket and walked to the house a short distance away. The other souls followed him. Calling it a house didn't really explain what it was. They didn't sleep, so there were no bedrooms. They didn't eat, so there was no kitchen. And as you probably deduced, there were no bathrooms or showers. There were no insects or bad weather, so windows were not necessary.

Tibus manifested a house made completely out of stone and crystals. It was majestic with beautiful colors. The stones were an assortment of colors and textures. He used his imagination to make it as beautiful as he could. There were about twenty rooms in the house, with each made out of different stones of various colors. Most of the rooms held large bookshelves filled with the Akashic records of souls whom he and his group were monitoring. The books were magical. Once opened, they would expand, creating an entire wall of information about a soul. Then the wall would come to life and show scenes from past and future lives. Anything you wanted to know about a soul was inside these books.

The souls followed Tibus into the house, and they formed into groups in the various rooms to do their work. Souls generally did not like to work alone on this dimension and preferred to work in groups. Sharing and being connected with others was considered the ideal way to live.

Giving back to the ALL, which is what life was known to be, was how souls preferred to live. The ALL, or All That Is, or the spirit of the Creator, was known and understood as the integrated oneness of all life. There was no separation between anything.

All consciousness coexisted as one consciousness. And nothing, absolutely nothing, could exist without being endowed with this consciousness.

The ALL was the source of consciousness for all life's existence. Once these souls had evolved to this level of spiritual understanding and knowing, all that mattered was the ALL. They were devoted to being in service to the ALL. Any thought or doubt contrary to this devotion did not exist. There was no human frailty in these souls, only one hundred percent devotion to the objective truth of their existence, and the truth of their connection to one another and to the Creator itself.

* * * * *

Zorka and Zade worked together in one of the rooms to analyze the lives of several volunteers on Earth. They had a book for each of the souls they were helping. Zorka took a book off one of the shelves and opened it onto a table. It was the Akashic record for Lindsay, a healer in Austin, Texas. She was a third-level old soul, born on October 29, 1977, and currently 36 years old. This made her a Six of Hearts, with a 36/9 lifepath. She was a Scorpio, with a Capricorn Moon, and Cancer rising. She was married with two sons, and her marriage was failing.

A Six of Hearts is a card of peace, harmony, and stability in love and family. It is about stability in relationships. However, for some Six of Hearts, they try to make a relationship work that is destined to fail, or they can act irresponsibly and sabotage it. Their lesson can be to understand what true love is about. They are strongly connected to the law of love, and what it takes to make love strong and lasting.[8]

Lindsay wanted the perfect love so desperately that she tried for years to make her relationship work. It was now becoming

---

8    Love Cards, Robert Camp, Sourcebooks Inc., 2004, p. 120.

obvious that it would not be. She had been miserable for the past few years. She wanted to change her life, but felt trapped. Her husband was somewhat content, and did not have the same desire to find more from his life.

A 36/9 is a powerful karmic path. They are drawn to understand the purpose of life, and life's higher calling. They are here to serve as examples of integrity, purity, and innocence. A 9 is a path about wisdom and maturity, and natural leadership. The 36 is a path of finding integrity. It is a difficult calling and requires reaching very high ideals. It can be a difficult mountain to climb.[9]

Lindsay was here to find love in her life and in her personal relationships, and then share her integrity with the world. To do that, she had to become deeply connected with her soul. She had to be led from within. Her love and wisdom had to come from within in order for her integrity to shine outward and be seen by all.

Zorka and Zade studied her current incarnation and past lives and understood what she needed. They made a decision and decided to put their ideas into action. They immediately moved their consciousness into Lindsay's space. They literally became entangled in her energy field. They could sense everything that Lindsay was sensing. They could read her mind and feelings. If you want an analogy, they were "wired in" completely to her awareness. Not one of her thoughts could be kept from them.

They were not the only spirit guides with Lindsay. She had two others currently with her, including her primary spirit guide, who had been with her since her incarnation into this body. Zade communicated with her two guides and told them what they wanted to do and why. The communication between discarnate beings was much easier than between humans. A huge amount of information could be transferred between discarnate souls in

---

9    The Life You Were Born To Live, Dan Millman, H J Kramer, 1993, p. 304.

seconds. And this information was understood and assimilated easily. Lindsay's primary guide agreed to let them proceed.

Zade and Zorka waited for an opportune time when Lindsay had finished an intense yoga class, and her mind was clear and quiet. They told her to leave her husband and begin a new journey. She had been thinking of leaving him for years, so this was not a new idea. However, this time they gave her the message with an intense feeling of emotion. Lindsay thought this was coming from herself, not knowing that Zade and Zorka were communicating to her.

Lindsay made up her mind to tell her husband that night. Zade and Zorka stayed with her and did not let her lose her nerve. After Lindsay got home and took a shower, they reminded her over and over to tell her husband tonight. As she dried herself with a towel and looked into the mirror, it was the only thing on her mind: "I'm going to tell him," she thought to herself. Then she went to make dinner, and the same thoughts permeated her brain. "This is it; I'm doing it tonight," she thought.

When Lindsay's husband got home from work, she told him their relationship was over. Zade and Zorka handed over the follow-up to her guides. They would help Lindsay find her new life. The next relationship she had would be with someone more compatible. The love of that relationship would lead her to become a better healer who was more passionate about helping others. Then her integrity would begin to shine through. Her sons would become awakened, and they, in turn, would influence their friends. Lindsay would impact her clients, friends, and family. The love of the Six of Hearts would reign and have a big impact. The world would be a better place because Lindsay had found her path.

\* \* \* \* \*

Zade and Zorka moved their consciousness back to Tibus' house on the 7th dimension. They put Lindsay's book back on the shelf and chose another. Her book was automatically updated to include the change they had helped make to Lindsay's life. These books were not the actual Akashic records, but had "links" to the originals. The actual Akashic records included the experiences of each soul in minute detail. Every soul had one, and they were not secrets or kept out of view. The Akashic records were the Creator's record book, and it was available for all to read.

\* \* \* \* \*

In separate rooms, the Tibus team was repeating what Zade and Zorka were doing. They did not have to stop to eat or sleep, so this continued at a constant pace unless they were interrupted by another concern.

In one of the rooms, Tibus was working by himself, although several souls were watching him and learning. He was studying the life of Peter, a 60-year-old writer in Santa Monica, California. His birthday was May 29, 1953, making him a Three of Clubs Gemini, with a 34/7 lifepath. The Three of Clubs was the writer's card, making him extremely gifted with the written word. Peter was also an old-soul volunteer who had come to help with the Earth's transition.

Peter's books were mostly about Gnostic spiritual philosophy, and he had self-published several, but his books were not selling. He had done a few lectures over the years, but they never propelled his book sales. Lately, he had lost his motivation to write or lecture. He lived alone and spent most of his time reading and waiting for the world to change. He knew there would soon be a spiritual transformation across the planet, and he even wanted to help, but he was stuck and didn't know how.

As a Three of Clubs, he was a natural teacher, but his tendency toward indecisiveness always sabotaged his thoughts of teaching. Being a natural business person as well, he could easily start a school and make it work, and he had a lot to offer. His gift was turning fear into faith, which was something that was direly needed at this time.[10]

As a 34/7, he was here to work through issues of trust, and to have faith in the spiritual process of life by finding practical ways to help others. His objective was to blend the expressiveness of a 3 with the practical nature of the 4. Also, the 7 meant he was close to his spirit. For an old soul, this usually leads a person to a process of self-discovery until they learn to trust. They can then become very expressive individuals, with a deep sense of knowing.[11]

Tibus knew what needed to be done. He immediately moved his consciousness into Peter's space and communicated with Peter's primary spirit guide. As usual, Tibus sent the spirit guide a large packet of information informing him why he was here and his intentions. The spirit guide was excited that Peter was going to be helped and agreed to allow Tibus to implement a change in Peter's life.

In Santa Monica, there was a new-age / metaphysical center that hosted lectures and classes. Tibus was aware of the center and knew that the owner was thinking of offering classes on ascension. This would be perfect for Peter and would give him a chance to help with Earth's transition.

Tibus knew that Peter was on their mailing list. He moved his consciousness into the owner's space and communicated with the owner's primary spirit guide. Then he telepathically told this spirit

---

10     Love Cards, Robert Camp, Sourcebooks Inc., 2004, p. 70.
11     The Life You Were Born To Live, Dan Millman, H J Kramer, 1993, p. 257.

guide the reason for his visit. The primary guide agreed to help. The plan was to create an ascension class and offer it to everyone on the mailing list.

When Peter received the flyer in the mail, Tibus made sure he attended. Peter had no idea where his desire to attend came from, but he felt it strongly. Peter felt that he needed to know what was being taught about ascension. Perhaps there was something he needed to know. After all, he had always felt a strong interest in both the planet's ascension and his own personal ascension. He had read a lot on the subject, but was always looking for more.

Peter had given a lecture before at the center and personally knew the owner. When he arrived to attend the class, they "coincidentally" ran into each other. The owner wanted to know what Peter was currently doing with his life, and was genuinely interested. Peter said that he had a lot of free time recently, and had come tonight to hear the ascension lecture.

The owner said he wanted to expand the lectures to Monday through Friday (not knowing that the idea had come from Tibus), but couldn't find enough teachers. Peter immediately said he was available (not knowing why he was so interested). The owner said the pay wouldn't be very good and was dependent on the number of students. Peter smiled and said he wasn't doing it for the money.

Tibus smiled to himself and knew his job was done here. He immediately moved himself back to his house on the 7th dimension.

\* \* \* \* \*

In another room, Semjase and Tamiel were working together. They each had a bookshelf that was full of the records of volunteers. Semjase decided to go first and picked a book of one of hers. It would take them months to get through the stack of books. Of course, there was no such thing as time here, but that did not negate how long it would take.

They opened the first book and began to look at Julie's life. She was an artist in Portland, Oregon. She was born on March 18, 1989, making her a Pisces and Five of Diamonds, with a 39/3 lifepath. They chose to make a change in her life when she was twenty-four years old in 2013. This was the first time in her life that they thought a change could have a significant impact.

All 5's are restless. They demand change in their life and get bored easily with the status quo. They dislike routine and adore freedom. Anything that limits their freedom will usually be eliminated or avoided. They have an inner sense of dissatisfaction that tends to make their jobs and relationships temporary. At the same time, they have a strong desire to help others and succeed when they align themselves to a higher purpose.[12]

As a 39/3, Julie was here to use her creativity in a process of cooperation and integrity, aligned with a higher purpose. It was inevitable that she would work with others as part of a team. And that she would have abundant energy and passion for her projects. The 9 gave her wisdom, and the 3 gave her expressiveness and emotional sensitivity.[13]

Semjase and Tamiel used this knowledge of Julie, as well as her numerology and astrology, along with her objectives for this incarnation, to form a plan to help her. They knew that she was an old-soul volunteer who came to help the planet raise its energy vibration. They also knew that she was falling behind many of the other volunteers of her age group. She was living at home and partying too much with her friends. She was an exceptional artist and an extremely creative person, but didn't know how to exploit her talent.

They found the perfect teammate that she needed, someone who would be a perfect mentor for her. Randy was a furniture maker who needed an artist to help him with designs that he

12      Love Cards, Robert Camp, Sourcebooks Inc., 2004, p. 110.
13      The Life You Were Born To Live, Dan Millman, H J Kramer, 1993, p. 162.

could carve into wood. He made beds (headboards and wooden frames), chairs, tables, dressers, and other furniture. He was very good, and his furniture sold well on the Internet.

The problem was that Randy lived near Seattle in the suburb of Bremerton. How could they arrange for the two to meet? They came up with a three-pronged plan. The first step would be to have one of Julie's friends become interested in his furniture. Next, they would get Julie and a friend to go to a concert in Seattle, where they could visit the furniture store. Lastly, they would have the furniture maker become aware of Julie's skill as an artist.

Semjase and Tamiel moved into Julie's space and connected with her primary spirit guide. They informed the guide of their task, which was accepted with enthusiasm. Once this was accomplished, they zeroed in on Julie's friend and nudged her to become obsessed with decorating her new apartment. She began to surf the Internet to find the perfect coffee table. She searched for "best coffee table" and found rave reviews for this guy in Bremerton, Washington. She didn't order it because it was beyond her budget, but she looked at his other stuff and was blown away by the quality. She spent an hour on his site looking at all of his furniture.

Next, an email was sent to Julie informing her that her favorite rock band, Death Cab for Cutie, was playing in Seattle in a couple of months. She loved this band and had to go. She called her friend, and they decided to do a road trip. Once they were on the road, her friend said that they had to go by this furniture maker in Bremerton so she could check out his coffee tables and his amazing furniture.

The day after the concert, they drove to Bremerton and went to see the furniture. Julie and her friend walked around the store and looked at all of the custom wood furniture. Julie noticed that the furniture was very unique and used a lot of creative designs. In many respects, they were pieces of art.

As they were walking out of the store, Julie noticed a sign that said "Artist Wanted." She thought it was odd to find such a sign.

She stopped and pointed at it, not knowing why she was getting emotional.

Her friend said, "Julie, you should ask about the job. This would be a cool place to work. This is some of the best custom furniture you can find."

Julie was silent, thinking to herself. This is where her Five of Diamonds card comes into play. She had been ready for something new for months, but could not find a good job. She thought this could be her ticket.

They turned around and went back to the front desk.

"I'm an artist, and I am interested in the job if you have one."

"Are you a good artist?" Randy asked.

"Mister," Julie's friend said, with a serious tone, "she is a better artist than anyone you will ever find. Can you get online?"

"I have an iPad."

"Perfect. Hand it over."

Randy entered his 4-digit password, and then passed the iPad to Julie's friend.

She entered an Internet URL where there were dozens of Julie's paintings.

"Check it out. She did all of these."

Randy scrolled through the paintings, not saying anything. Then he stopped and whistled. "Whoa, you are good. Why do you want to work here?"

"I like your furniture, and I need a job."

"Okay, then. I'll start you at forty-thousand a year, plus medical and dental. If you are good and the furniture sells, you will get a nice raise and profit sharing. I have three other employees, and I don't do this just to make money for myself. I live very simply. Here we all share in the profits, and I give a good portion to charity and friends. This business is about giving back to society and humanity."

Julie smiled and held out her hand. "Just the kind of place where I want to work. You now have an artist on the payroll!"

Randy smiled. "Welcome aboard."

What Julie didn't know was that the owner was an old-soul metaphysician who would mentor her into becoming a highly spiritual person very quickly. Moreover, their teamwork would lead to some of the most beautiful furniture one could purchase.

Semjase and Tamiel immediately went back to the 7th dimension and the room in Tibus' house where they had been working previously. Instead of celebrating a successful intervention, Tamiel took another book from the shelf, and they proceeded to help the next volunteer.

# Chapter Five

# MORE VOLUNTEERS

Lori was an energy healer in Sedona. She was both a Reiki master and practitioner of Reconnective Healing, which she had learned from Eric Pearl.[14] Lori was a Seven of Spades, and was born on February 5, 1963. This made her an Aquarius, with a 26/8 lifepath.

The Seven of Spades is perhaps the most spiritual card you can have. And anyone who is a Seven of Spades has an abundance of wisdom. One negative for this card is that health issues are inevitable if they do not live by higher values. One might say this card mandates that these individuals live by the highest moral values, or else they will get sick. Their illnesses make them look within and develop faith. On a positive note, if they live those higher values, their wishes usually come true because they are blessed. They are protected, and nothing can hurt them except their own fears and doubts.[15]

As a 26/8 lifepath, Lori had strength and inherent power. Anyone who has an 8 lifepath generally obtains abundance and power in some form. They are usually blessed with the strength to achieve their desires. A 26/8 is here to obtain and share their abundance in the service of others. They are also here to be in alignment with the highest ideals, which is in correlation to the Seven of Spades. Many who have this card have an inner conflict of assuming the power that they hold. Eventually, they come to learn to assert themselves and gain recognition.[16]

---

14    www.thereconnection.com
15    Love Cards, Robert Camp, Sourcebooks Inc., 2004, p. 150.
16    The Life You Were Born To Live, Dan Millman, H J Kramer, 1993, p. 270.

Lori, just like everyone else in the world, fit her card and lifepath. She was fifty years old and had gone through several debilitating illnesses during her life. As a child, she'd had Lyme disease; in her twenties, chronic fatigue syndrome. Currently, she was living with type 2 diabetes. She was a gifted healer and had a busy practice. Many people drove from the Phoenix area for her services.

You would think, since she was living in the new-age capital of the U.S., Lori would be on a solid spiritual path. However, her diet had been poor most of her life. It was the diet of mainstream America with too much meat, sugar, and processed foods. She was fifty pounds overweight, and her energy level was somewhat depleted, leaving her tired at the end of the day.

She needed to take charge of her life and get healthy. This was holding her back from reaching her potential. She knew her life was not what she wanted it to be, but she was stuck in a rut. One day a friend recommended a book by Dolores Cannon, entitled The Convoluted Universe. This is a series of books, and her friend advised her to begin with Book Three. Lori read Book Three and loved it. She talked with her friend about the book and how she would like to do a past life regression. Her friend mentioned that there was someone in Sedona who did LBL (life between life) regressions.

This is where the spirit guides come into play. Little did Lori know that this change was instigated by Turel and Silas, who were working from Tibus' house on the 7th dimension. It was no accident that Dolores' book had made its way into Lori's hands.

During the LBL regression, Lori's higher self explained to her that she did not need to have diabetes, nor did she need to feel tired. These could easily be solved by eating more raw foods, and abstaining from most meat and processed foods. A healthier diet, along with a more positive outlook on life, could easily transform her life.

Her higher self went on to add that Lori was a child of light – an advanced old soul – who had a lot to offer humanity. Her healing abilities could increase tenfold if she became more in tune with her soul, and this would not be that difficult to achieve. Lori had already been a metaphysical student for most of her life. All she needed to do was take it more seriously. She needed to rise each morning with the intent to connect with her soul, and then remain balanced and centered the entire day. She needed to become more reverent and grateful for her life, and to become humble and give back to humanity. In all areas of her life, she was to be an example, and hold the highest moral values. She was to live a life of integrity and gratitude. She was not only capable of this; it was her destiny. It was as natural for her as falling in love.

When the regression was over, Lori had an epiphany. She wondered why she hadn't been living this way her entire life. "I've been the proverbial fool," she thought. "Well, that's enough. I'm going to change my life. No longer am I going to just be an energy healer. Now I am going to be a spiritual energy healer. I'm going to hold the energy that my patients want. I'm going to set an example."

Within a few months, Lori changed her life. She lost fifty pounds from eating only healthy food, and her diabetes cured itself. Her energy levels increased dramatically, and she literally vibrated at a higher frequency. Her morning meditations put her in sync with her soul, and she remained closely connected to her soul throughout the day. In many respects, she was an incarnate angel walking the planet. Those who came to see her always smiled and knew they were lucky to have her as their healer. She brought about cures that many would consider miraculous.

Lori came into her power and abundance. She knew that her lifestyle was not only good for herself, but that it was also good for humanity. She knew that she was helping and giving back. Now that her awareness had expanded to recognize her impact on humanity, she wanted to do more. So, she went online to Meetup. com and found groups she could join. She wanted to network with like-minded people and see if there were other ways she could give back. She could no longer stay home and watch from the sidelines as society faltered. That was no longer an acceptable way to live her life. After she had her LBL session, she knew it was her destiny to play a part in the positive evolution of humanity.

All this happened from two spirit guides putting a book in her hands.

\*   \*   \*   \*   \*

Tom's life was a bit of a mess. He was a tour guide in Glastonbury, England and an alcoholic. Not a full-blown alcoholic, but a functioning alcoholic who got drunk nearly every night. Somehow he managed to get to work each day. Luckily, the tour guide business did not require him to wake up early in the morning.

When he was younger, he had studied history in college, and became enchanted with England's past, especially its ancient past. As he would later learn, Tom was an old soul volunteer who had been a Druid in more than one past life. This explained the kinship he felt with the Glastonbury and Cornwall regions of Southwest England. His love of the local history, his penchant for drinking, and his dislike of working an 8-to-5 job, led him to become a tour guide. It fit his talents, interests, and his lifestyle.

Tom was an Ace of Clubs, born on October 21, 1968. That made him a Libra with a 28/10 lifepath. As an Ace of Clubs, he had an insatiable desire for knowledge, along with a strong need for love. An Ace of Clubs abhor being alone and seems to always to be searching for the ideal romantic partner. Their curiosity makes them avid students. They tend to be smart, with excellent communication skills. There is a spiritual side to this card, and they must turn to spirituality later in life or else find themselves dissatisfied.[17]

As a 28/10 lifepath, Tom was blessed with creativity, sensitivity, strength, expression, and intuition. As he matured, he was likely to be in a position of authority with abundant resources. However, this could only happen if he gained a modicum of self-confidence and a motive of service.[18]

As a Libra and an Ace of Clubs, he was a voracious reader and read twice as fast as the average person. His small apartment was littered with books. He would read on his days off when he did not have any tours, but inevitably he ended up at the pub at night. Nearly all of his advertising was done via the Internet, but he did have a connection with a shop in Glastonbury that displayed flyers of his services. He also was referred by several locals to the myriad of tourists. His business was always brisk.

Tom had lost the love of his life to cancer when she was in her late twenties. This was part of what drove him to drink. At night he felt lonely, but he refused to find someone to replace her. He'd had a few girlfriends, but they could not get close to his heart. He had given that to his wife.

He lived his life in a very simple manner. He read about history and Gnostic spirituality, and gave his tours during the day. Then at night he would drink at the pub. Year after year, he continued this pattern. He was stuck.

Semjase and Tamiel looked at Tom's life and knew they had to do something dramatic to get him to change. They decided to have him invited to a local group that met once a month to hear a local channeler. This channeler was channeling Archangel Michael, and profound knowledge was being shared with the group. Their plan was two-pronged. First, they would get him invited and convince

---

17      Love Cards, Robert Camp, Sourcebooks Inc., 2004, p. 34.
18      The Life You Were Born To Live, Dan Millman, H J Kramer, 1993, p. 117.

him to attend. Second, they would have Archangel Michael make sure he returned and become a regular member of the group.

One night at the pub, a friend of Tom's mentioned that his wife had been attending monthly channelings. Lately, the channeler had been telling the group about the local history of Glastonbury. The friend's wife had been so fascinated that she couldn't stop talking about it: Mary Magdalene, Mother Mary, Joseph of Arimathea, the Mary and Michael ley lines, et cetera.

Tom became intrigued and mentioned that he wouldn't mind learning more about the local history. He asked his friend to find out whether he could attend the next meeting. Since Tom was a well-known local tour guide and a historian, the group was happy to have him join. Once the channeling started, it didn't take long for Archangel Michael to speak directly to Tom.

"Who have we here tonight? Ladies and gentlemen, we have a 5th-level old soul in our company. Thank you for coming, Tom. You may not know this, but you have lived in Glastonbury before, in ancient times. The history that I speak of, you were a part of. In fact, you are here today to help others remember, and to help humanity raise its vibration. You are one of the volunteers.

"We ask that you continue to come to these monthly meetings so that you will begin to remember why you incarnated. It is important that you begin to follow a spiritual path so that you can show others the way. You are blessed with an inner strength and clear intuition. Your link to your soul is much stronger than you know. With a little bit of effort, not only can you find your soul, but you can share it with everyone who comes on your tours of this region.

"More than that, you can begin writing so that the pilgrims who come to Glastonbury can take back with them the truth of the ancient Gnostics. You can sell them a short book that can transform many of their lives. This book will be the story of Glastonbury and the history of the ancients. I know you can write it, but before you begin, I ask that you attend at least six sessions and curtail your drinking. At that time, you will be ready."

Tom was mesmerized. He had wanted to write a book about the ancient times of Glastonbury for many years, but never started it. He also knew deep in his heart that he was strongly connected to this land, and now he knew why. Lastly, he was looking for a reason to change his life, but had never found it. Now he had. He felt a new invigoration for life. He was ready for a new journey.

*　*　*　*　*

Kevin was a musician in Chicago. He was married, and his wife was the primary provider. She had allowed him to pursue his career in music for many years. However, he was now 35 years old, and his career had never been anything more than low paying gigs. He played keyboards and sang, and was very good, but it never took him anywhere.

Kevin was born on May 8, 1973. This made him a Taurus and a Jack of Diamonds, with 33/6 lifepath. As a Taurus, he preferred spending most of his time at home, and as a fixed sign, he did not like change.

As a Jack of Diamonds, he was sharp, clever, with a large quantity of wit and charm. This likeability quality, along with his musical talent, is what made it possible for him to remain in a band for so many years. He was also blessed with a quick and creative mind, which was always appreciated by others. Many Jack of Diamonds make a living in the entertainment industry or as psychics. As is common with many Jacks, they tend to live their life by having fun. For this reason, they tend to be self employed.[19]

With a 33/6 lifepath, Kevin was destined to work on issues of perfectionism (becoming a professional musician) and emotional expression (singing in public). People with this lifepath tend to

19    Love Cards, Robert Camp, Sourcebooks Inc., 2004, p. 218.

have very high ideals and are keenly sensitive to when others are not living up to these high standards. But they often experience self-doubt about what they are truly supposed to do. In fact, their job is to inspire others to live up to higher standards and ideals; to use their talent to provide an inspiring vision to the world.[20]

Being a Taurus, Kevin was stubborn and knew that playing music and enjoying life was a good option for him. He knew that his other options were less attractive. In fact, he couldn't think of what else he wanted to do. The world depressed him, but he couldn't think of a way to make it better other than playing music. However, he also knew that playing in a band that made very little money was becoming problematic and creating stress in his marriage. It was unlikely he could do this his entire life. At some point, he was going to have to find something else to do.

Zade and Zorka looked over Kevin's life and agreed that the best choice was to turn him into a professional channeler. With Kevin's quick brain and high intelligence, they knew that he could easily turn it into a self-employed business. They also knew that he had read many books that were channeled and would be comfortable accepting communication from the other side.

The first thing they had to do was to find a discarnate soul who would channel through Kevin. They went into his energetic field and informed his primary spirit guide of their intentions. Then they asked if the guide knew of a soul who might want to come through Kevin. The guide recommended the Arcturians because of Kevin's affinity to their deep spirituality. Many Arcturians were monitoring Earth's transition, and there should be several who could come through Kevin. Zade and Zorka agreed to contact several Arcturians and make an agreement.

Being a new-ager and a Gnostic, Kevin attended spiritual fairs from time to time. His wife liked to go as well, and it was

---

20    The Life You Were Born To Live, Dan Millman, H J Kramer, 1993, p. 237.

always her idea that they attend. He was usually comfortable staying home, but she dragged him out of the house on occasion. One weekend they went to a fair, and Kevin felt drawn to have a 30-minute Tarot reading.

Once the reading began, the reader grew quiet and looked seriously at Kevin. "Oh my, you have a new path to go down. You are to begin channeling the Arcturians. They are around you and are waiting for you to call them in."

Kevin laughed. "Seriously? How do you know that?"

"I'm not just a Tarot reader. I'm also a medium and can communicate with the other side. They are with you right now. It seems like you have some kind of agreement with them to bring their information to the public."

This time Kevin did not laugh. He became very quiet and serious. "What else can you tell me?"

The Tarot reader turned over some cards. "This is a pivotal moment for you. A new career, a new direction. Completely transformational. Your life is about to change dramatically for the better. You are being blessed here. You are being called. Feel honored. Feel reverent."

Kevin nodded. "The Arcturians are from a 5$^{th}$ dimensional planet. Are you picking that up?"

"Yes," the reader said. "They are highly evolved. The knowledge you are about to receive is needed at this time of the Earth's awakening."

"How do I do this channeling?" Kevin asked.

The reader turned over more cards. "Go to a class where they teach channeling is my advice. I think one weekend is all you need and then you will be able to do it. I'm picking up that it should be fairly easy for you."

Kevin nodded. "Thank you. You have been very helpful."

"I feel honored," replied the reader. "You are being led in a very good direction. It feels good to be able to help you."

Kevin got up to leave, and the reader handed him his card. "If you begin channeling, please contact me and let me know where I can obtain the information. I have a feeling it is going to be extraordinary."

Kevin took the card. "I'll do that."

The Tarot reader smiled. "Thanks."

Kevin quickly found his wife and told her about his incredible reading. He said he was going to find a channeling class and see if he could channel the Arcturians.

She was ecstatic and supported his decision enthusiastically. She had been waiting for him to find something to be passionate about other than music. She was ready for him to pursue something new. Little did she know that her spirit guides were giving her these thoughts so that when this moment came, she would support his decision. Her support fortified Kevin's decision to take the class, and helped with his transition into a new career.

Soon after, he began channeling the Arcturians and taping the information. His wife even helped when she was home from work. He built a website and began selling his channelings on the Internet. Then he began doing lectures and performing live public channelings. In very little time, his life had transformed, and he was no longer interested in playing music professionally. He was now a channel. Being a Jack of Diamonds, he was a natural performer. This allowed him to speak in public in a very dynamic way. He spoke to his audience before channeling and explained what the Arcturians were teaching. This tended to enhance the messages that were channeled and impacted many people who came to listen. He had become not only a channeler, but a teacher.

\* \* \* \* \*

Mary was a substance abuse counselor in Tucson, Arizona. She was a Sagittarius, born on December 19, 1973, and a Queen of Hearts, with a 32/5 lifepath. She was 38 years old and had two kids in high school from a long ago divorce. She never remarried and had perpetual financial issues. Her desire to help others led her to do an assortment of different jobs that were never well-paying. She never wanted a career, which is common for advanced old souls. Material wealth never appealed to her. She always followed her heart, which was huge, being a Queen of Hearts.

As a Sagittarius, she was perpetually happy. She was also a Pisces rising and had an abundance of water in her chart. This made her a very sensitive, loving person. However, as a fire sign, she did have an occasional temper flare. These never lasted long and were quickly extinguished. She did have a philosophical streak, and liked reading historical books about the Gnostics, such as those by Margaret Starbird and Elaine Pagels.

As a Queen of Hearts, she was extremely idealistic with a degree of charm that attracted other people to her warm heart. Those born on a Queen of Hearts day (July 29, August 27, September 25, October 23, November 21, and December 19), are the mothers of love, and they share this love with all those they meet. It is the perfect card for motherhood, and Mary was a devoted mother who enjoyed a strong relationship with her two daughters. A Queen of Hearts is always talented and can achieve great feats if they focus on their high ideals.[21]

With a 32/5 lifepath, Mary was very focused on her personal freedom. She could be a devoted mother, but she couldn't give her freedom away to a career or a relationship. Ironically, while those on a 32/5 lifepath cherish their freedom, they are drawn to work with others in cooperation. They want to be a team player.

---

21    Love Cards, Robert Camp, Sourcebooks Inc., 2004, p. 228.

In Mary's case, this was to find a way to cooperate with others in order to help humanity. She was willing to give nearly all of herself ,as long as her freedom was not lost, in the pursuit of cooperation to achieve her life goal.[22]

Tibus had a personal affinity with Mary. He admired how she lived her life outside of the mainstream, yet worked within it to help advance humanity. Mary was not someone who received a lot of admiration, because she worked in the trenches doing low-paying jobs that most people shied away from. She did not seek the limelight or recognition. Yet, she was highly intelligent and talented. Most people who knew her considered her choices as a waste of her talent. They also thought that she was making both her life, and her children's lives, more difficult than necessary.

Tibus wanted to help Mary, but he didn't want to disrupt the life that she had created. Mary was doing her part to help humanity. However, many of those she was interacting with were not likely to awaken spiritually. Mary was helping people to carry on with their lives. This was positive, but she was not helping with Earth's transformation. This is what Tibus wanted her to achieve.

He decided to make her a healer, not just any healer, but a miraculous healer. She would use her hands and inner-sight to heal thousands of people. And her healing prowess would lead to both physical and spiritual healing. Once she obtained her healing powers, her spirituality would blossom and infect many of her clients.

Mary was leaving the prison after another day of counseling inmates who had substance abuse problems, when she suddenly thought about becoming a massage therapist. It was an ongoing thought that she could not get out of her mind the past few days. The state of Arizona was offering to pay for six months of job

---

22      The Life You Were Born To Live, Dan Millman, H J Kramer, 1993, p. 210.

training for low-income households for the job of their choice. She had been working part-time at the prison, and easily qualified.

"Why not?" she thought. "I can be both a counselor and a massage therapist. After all, I have plenty of time for training. If they are going to pay for my classes, I might as well do it." On the way home, she stopped by the government agency and filled out the forms. A few weeks later, she received a letter in the mail accepting her application. She signed up for a 500-hour course (the requirement in Arizona to become licensed) and was soon a licensed massage therapist.

Once she began doing massage therapy, she read about energy healing and how it could be used in conjunction with massage therapy. She began offering both massage therapy and energy healing. She had such good results that soon she was spending more time doing energy healing than massage. Eventually she stopped doing counseling at the prison and focused all of her time working at home as a healer and massage therapist.

Mary became, for lack of a better word, a new-ager. A better word would be a lightworker. She started honing her spiritual path and living a lifestyle of high moral values and high ideals. She was an example that others could follow. When someone stepped into her house, the energy was that of total love. She exuded it as a Queen of Hearts, and also as someone who walked the talk. Her house was filled with crystals, incense, angels, fairies, and other new-age paraphernalia. It was decorated mostly in white and exuded harmony and integrity. It was the home of someone who knew about the spiritual side of life. There was no falsity here. It was total truth and an awareness of what is true and real.

Word spread of Mary's healing prowess. She had many clients, old and new. She created a library of metaphysical books that she shared with clients. She even had a large sign near her library of books. It had a big question mark, along with the question, "Have you read these? Please take one. They are free!"

Mary did not want a new house, or a new car. She wanted to give back to humanity. The more books she could give away, the more she smiled. Her smile was so warm and loving that when you accepted one of her free books, you felt compelled to read it. Many of her customers would get a new book each time they came to see her for a massage or healing. Often they would bring back the books they had read, and Mary would give them away again. Her goal was to give away a thousand books, and it was likely to happen.

Here is the list of books that she kept in her library:

### The Convoluted Universe (Book 3)

*By Dolores Cannon*

Knowledge obtained through hypnotic regression. There are four books in the series, but start with Book 3, which is the best.

### Journey of Souls

*Channeled by Michael Newton*

Perhaps the best book ever written on life in the spirit world. If you have any interest on why we're here, this is a must read.

### The New Revelations

*Channeled by Neale Donald Walsch*

Spiritual philosophy. Question and answer sessions with God.

### The Disappearance of the Universe

*Channeled by Gary Renard*

This book is fascinating and controversial. It is the product of two beings from the spiritual plane who appeared to Gary. These beings came to clarify the Course in Miracles. What they have to say is well worth reading.

### Anna, Grandmother of Jesus

*Channeled by Claire Heartsong*

An incredible history of Jesus' life and his family. Perhaps the best book of its kind.

## Anastasia (The Ringing Cedars Series)

*by Vladimir Megre*

An incredible series of books. I don't know if Anastasia is real, but the material is original and insightful. In fact, it is changing people's lives.

## Krishnamurti - Think On These Things

*by D. Rajagopal (editor)*

Spiritual philosophy. Speeches given by Krishnamurti in the 1960s. He was one of the most enlightened beings of the 20th century (my opinion).

## A New Earth

*by Eckhart Tolle*

A stunning book written by a human. Spiritual material of this depth is usually channeled. Tolle understands the ego as well as anyone alive today.

## We The Arcturians

*Channeled by Norma Milanovich*

This book is powerful. Are you interested in what the Arcturians, who live in the 5th Dimension, think about spirituality? Or, why they are here watching us?

## The Serpent of Light

*Channeled by Drunvalo Melchizedek*

Do you want to know what 2012 is really all about? This book is for you. I'll give you a hint: it is why the Arcturians are here.

## The Kingdom

*Channeled by Paul Selig*

Perhaps the best channeled material I have ever read. It explains how to connect with your soul. I would only recommend it for old souls.

# Chapter Six

# THE HEALING CENTERS

Mestos was troubled. He was analyzing the future timelines, and he didn't like what he was seeing. There was too much potential for chaos and disorder when the world's economies began to falter. He had to do something that would ameliorate the outcome. He mentally called Sampson to come see him.

Sampson appeared before him as a semitransparent manifestation in a flowing white robe. They were both inside a crystal building that was as clear as glass.

"Sampson, I have another project that I need you to organize. I've been analyzing the future timelines on Earth, and everything is progressing very well and is on schedule for ascension. However, some of the timelines are extremely chaotic, with governments becoming overly aggressive and constraining demonstrators. In America, there is the potential for widespread arrests and prolonged confinements at detention centers. It is disturbing, and not the outcome we want to manifest."

"What would you like me to do, Mestos?"

"I think we can reduce the potential for chaos if we create a new alternative way of living. One way would be to build a few communities that are centered on holistic healing centers. These can be small communities of evolved souls that show the way. They can provide miracle healings and also be an example of a new community that provides hope. This hope could diffuse the anger and frustration that will become prevalent. If America creates an alternative way of living, then the rest of the world will follow. We need America to take the lead and show the way."

"I think I understand what you want," Sampson said. "You want these healing centers to be beacons of hope that others can emulate. They are to be exemplary examples of the possibility of a new way of life. And you want them to be populated with many of the highly evolved volunteers."

Mestos nodded. "That is exactly what I want."

"You want them in place by 2025?" Sampson asked.

"Yes, that would be a good time frame. Build three of them in the western portion of the United States. Include at least one exceptionally gifted healer in each location, and give them plenty of financing. I want them to thrive so that others will take notice and reproduce what they start."

Sampson nodded. "How many people do you want at each location?"

"Let's keep them small at first, perhaps thirty to a hundred. Once they are built, it is likely they will grow in size."

"And since these are to be the examples for people to emulate," Sampson said, "you want them to uphold exemplary spiritual values and reverence for the planet and humanity."

Mestos smiled. "I think you have it figured out. I want them to become widely known and respected as models for a new way of life. They should be self-sufficient and sustainable, but more than anything else, independent and free."

"I like this plan, Mestos. You are going to give people an alternative way to live. That way instead of rebelling and demonstrating against the crumbling state of affairs, they can simply start over using this new paradigm."

"Yes," Mestos replied. "These new communities will give people hope. If they can see an alternative to their current situation, they will take it. Also, it will diffuse the negative energy that builds in the large inner cities. Instead of anger and frustration building to a crescendo, these healing centers, and new modes of living, will provide an outlet that will be needed. In many respects, the healing centers will act as a pressure valve, releasing the buildup of energy before it explodes."

Sampson nodded. "Indeed, if the people remain calm, then so will the authorities, and vice versa. If the people riot, the authorities will have a reason to become belligerent."

"Exactly," Mestos said. "We can't eliminate chaos, but we can limit it. The more people we can influence to calmly leave their cities and start a new way of life, the better."

Sampson nodded. "I understand what is needed."

＊　＊　＊　＊　＊

Sampson called forth a council to organize the three healing centers. It was held on the 7th dimension and was composed of twenty-two souls. This time the meeting was arranged around a circular pattern. There was no table in the middle, but there were chairs. The chairs were symbolic because they were all in their light bodies and could not feel them. Nor did they speak vocally. As was the norm on the spiritual planes, communication took place via telepathy and energy transference. Nothing was hidden between souls. All life was one consciousness that was shared.

After everyone was assembled, which only required a matter of seconds, Sampson began the meeting.

"Thank you all for coming. You have been selected because you are exemplary soul guides. As you know from reading my energy, this has to do with project Earth Awaken and Mestos. He is pleased with your work helping the volunteers on Earth make progress to raising the vibration of the planet and strengthening the crystalline grid.

"Now he has another project he would like you to implement. Instead of describing the project or explaining why it is needed, I am simply going to begin by telling you what he wants done.

"Form three teams to build three healing centers in the western portion of the United States. Each healing center should be populated with thirty to a hundred people. They should hold the highest values for humanity with the goal of sustaining and expanding those values. Also, include at least one gifted healer in each center who is capable of healing any ailment. Make these centers successful and well-known throughout the United States as beacons of hope."

Sampson paused and waited for a reply. He looked out at all of the members of the council who shimmered in their light bodies.

"Why not let them figure this out for themselves using their free will?" one of the council members asked.

"Mestos is concerned," Sampson replied, "that ascension and the strengthening of the crystalline grid could be impacted by a rise in discord. He wants to ensure that people have an option besides revolt and dissension."

"He is impinging on their free will," another council member said. "He could be changing their destiny."

"I understand your concern," Sampson continued. "We normally do not impact free will this directly. However, because of the importance of ascension and what it will mean to the entire universe, Mestos has made an exception."

Sampson waited for another comment.

"I don't have a problem with this approach," said one of the council members. "These healing centers and self-sustaining communities were going to happen anyway. We are just going to spur them on."

"Exactly," Sampson said. "Mestos just wants to ensure they are in place before the protests and revolt begins in America.

There is the potential for widespread disruptions, which could feed on itself and make it very difficult for people to overcome their fears. We need to give them hope and confidence before the demonstrations begin. If a few examples are in place, then people will see an alternative to their way of life. Instead of demanding that problems are fixed, they will simply begin anew. We want people to look towards the future and a new way of life."

"How far is Mestos going to go to ensure that the New Earth comes into being?" asked another council member. "Is this the last project? Or will there be more?"

"He did not say," Sampson replied. "He has been studying the timelines since we began our efforts to help the volunteers. After we build the healing centers, he will study them again. Hopefully, this will be all that is required."

Sampson paused, and there were no more questions.

"We need to form three teams. I would like each of you to volunteer to be on a team. The first seven on my left will be one team, the first seven on my right will be another, and the remaining will form the final team. Meet with your teams after we adjourn and discuss how you would like to proceed. I would recommend selecting a home base where you can work from, and then immediately proceed to that location to begin this project. I will be the overall leader of the project for coordination. If anyone has any questions, come to me. I will be monitoring your progress."

Sampson paused to see if there was a question. "Unless anyone has any questions, I think our meeting is concluded."

Sampson's light body dissolved, and he was gone.

*　*　*　*　*

Tibus was on the council. He looked at his fellow teammates and informed them that he had a perfect place where they could work. He gave them a mental image of his house, and they quickly agreed it was ideal. They quickly moved their light bodies to this location and had a meeting to discuss how to proceed.

Tibus was well known, and he was quickly deferred to as the team leader. The other six teammates were seated in Tibus' work room. Tibus stood before them and explained how he had been working on Mestos' project to help the volunteers and had several people in his house working on the project. Some of them would likely help them work on creating the healing center.

On one of the walls, a large screen came to life and displayed a real-time image of Pagosa Springs, a location in southern Colorado.

"This is my first choice," Tibus said. "It is already a healing town, with their hot springs. It is isolated in an unpopulated area and has 300 days of sunshine each year. The elevation is high at 7,000 feet, but there is plenty of water. The highs in the winter are usually in the 40s. I think the climate is acceptable."

"It is beautiful there," one of the teammates said.

"Yes, it is," replied Tibus. "I have an affinity with nature and the beauty of nature. This location will keep me motivated to succeed."

One of the teammates laughed. "Tibus, that has never been one of your weaknesses. You are one of the hardest-working souls I know."

Tibus smiled. "Perhaps you are right. I will work hard no matter what location we choose."

"This location is fine," one of the teammates replied. "Southern Colorado is a good choice. Does anyone have an objection or another site we should look at?"

There was silence, and so it was agreed upon.

"Let's brainstorm how we can make this healing center come into being," Tibus said.

One of the teammates quickly said, "First, we need to give someone the idea to build a healing center and the finances to achieve it."

"I have that taken care of," Tibus replied. "There is an advanced soul near Portland who has been planning this for years. She has a couple of things blocking her, but this is her dream. She already has at least five friends who are healers and would like to join her. All she has been waiting for is her spirit to guides to show her to the location."

Tibus changed the screen to show this woman in real-time at her house near Portland. "This is Charlene. She is a Queen of Clubs with a bright mind and a wealth of wisdom. She is highly evolved and an excellent healer. She has been preparing for this her whole life. She can hardly function in society because she is so closely aligned with spirit. In fact, she journeys out of her body nearly every night."

The other teammates had the ability to mentally tap into Charlene's Akashic records and learn about her. It only took them a few seconds to see how perfect she would be as one of the leaders of this healing center.

One of the teammates spoke. "I see that she has been planning this for years with several of her close friends."

Tibus nodded. "Yes, this won't be hard to implement. Let's talk about how the healing center will be organized."

"Well," one of the teammates said, "they already have a general idea on how they want to build it. They got the idea from Archangel Michael using sacred geometry. The buildings are to be built in a circular pattern, each a specific distance from the other. In the center is the main building, which is the actual healing center. Then they plan to use crystal stones to create a vortex of positive energy. This was all outlined in a book that was channeled by Archangel Michael."

"Yes," another teammate added. "One of her friends actually keeps this book open on his bookshelf to remind him of what needs to be done. The general design has already been decided. The only unknown is how large to build the circle of homes and the sizes of the homes. However, they were looking into purchasing pre-built houses that look like real homes, only are much smaller. These would be ideal and easy to install."

"Another friend of hers," said another teammate, "has an idea for the design of the healing center. It is firmly planted in his mind. We can use those plans and give them ideas for a few beneficial changes."

Tibus nodded. "I think with all of this pre-planning by Charlene and her friends, the design of the healing center should be easy to accomplish. Also, the social structure should be easy to form. They already have an objective of including only aware old souls and their family and friends. They want it to be a harmonious place where love thrives. I don't think that will be difficult to achieve."

"We can help them to build a large garden with several greenhouses," one of the teammates added. "Windmills and solar panels to provide energy will be a natural fit. We need to find them a location with an abundant water well."

The screen changed and displayed a location with a For Sale sign. "Here is fifty acres for sale just outside of Pagosa Springs," One of the teammates said. "The water table here is very good and shallow. They can easily drill a well. It is in a meadow, and the soil is excellent. Plus, there is a nearby road that has a power line that they can tie into through the local government."

Tibus smiled. "This is ideal. We have found our healing center."

There was silence as everyone agreed that this would be the site.

"Now that we have found the site and have a general idea of how to build it, let's talk about the people who will join Charlene and her friends," Tibus said. "Who wants to find a couple of old-soul handymen who can build and fix nearly anything?"

"I will volunteer for that," one of the teammates replied. "I have someone in mind who is incarnate that I know."

Tibus nodded. "Who wants to find two people who are highly successful, yet willing to move to a healing center? Ideally, they would be self-employed, such as a writer, artist, or musician. They need to be willing to support the healing center with their income."

"I will volunteer for that," one of the teammates replied. "I think I know a few souls who might be a good fit."

Tibus nodded. "Let's try to find about twenty people for the initial group, and then it will likely double in size from its success. I will work with Charlene to connect with as many of her healing friends as possible. I think I can get seven or eight to join her. I need the rest of you to find about eight souls who would like to live at the healing center, and have some type of connection to Charlene and her friends."

"How are you going to get Charlene to come here and purchase the property?" one of the teammates asked Tibus.

"It shouldn't be difficult," Tibus replied. "The first step will be to manifest some money to build the center. One of her friends likely has a connection to money that we can utilize. The second step will be to guide her to southern Colorado to look for a location."

"We need one last thing," Tibus said, "before we adjourn and begin our work. I need someone to find an extraordinary healer who can heal any human ailment."

"I will find someone," replied one of the teammates.

"Perfect," Tibus said. "Then we are ready to begin. If anyone has any questions, then come and find me."

\* \* \* \* \*

Charlene was ecstatic with joy. She literally could not stop feeling good. It was as if her ability to generate endorphins was nonstop. Margie, one of her closest friends, had inherited five million dollars, and she wanted to give it to Charlene to build her healing center. They had talked about it numerous times over the years, and now that she had the money in her bank account, that was how she wanted to spend it. She wanted to quit her job and help Charlene build the healing center as soon as possible.

Charlene agreed, but first they had to find a location. For some unknown reason, the only place that Charlene wanted to look was in southern Colorado. They decided to do a road trip and try to find a place.

They drove to Cortez and Durango and checked out properties for sale in the area. Everywhere they looked, it didn't quite feel right. Then they moved on to Pagosa Springs, and the third town was the charm. Charlene instantly fell in love with a plot of land on 50 acres nestled in a meadow near some mountains. She knew this was it. She felt it deep inside to the same degree as when she first heard Margie say that she had the money for the healing center. It felt right.

She smiled and spun herself in a circle with outstretched arms. "This is it! We can build it right here!"

Margie smiled and began dialing the phone number on the For Sale sign. "Is the property on Dawson Road still for sale?"

Charlene watched as Margie listened intently.

"What is the price?" Margie asked.

Margie listened for the answer and then said, "Three thousand dollars per acre, for a total of one hundred and fifty thousand dollars, plus a three percent commission? Great, does it come with water rights?"

Charlene watched as Margie nodded while listening.

"The water table is low, so we shouldn't have any problem drilling a well. Okay, this is exactly what we were looking for.

Will you take a check? How long will it take to get the paperwork in order?"

Charlene smiled. It was happening.

"Great. We will meet you at 2 p.m. to sign the papers at the bank. Bye."

They hugged. "It's ours!"

\*   \*   \*   \*   \*

Once they got back to Portland, they both began making phone calls to their close friends. They informed them that they were going to build the healing center, and would like them to be a part of it. They knew that this was a major change and that most of their friends would likely turn down the offer at this time, but would perhaps come later. Surprisingly, they found four friends and their families who were ready to move immediately.

Charlene told them that she wanted to first build a few houses and the main healing center before anyone could move in. This would take at least a year to complete. She and Margie would do this by themselves, along with Connor, a lifelong friend who had always wanted to help build the center.

Charlene and Connor were both highly intelligent Aquarians (born in early February) and skilled in many areas. Margie was a Capricorn with strong leadership skills. The three of them made a very capable team. Plus, they were all old souls with vast amounts of wisdom. Charlene and Connor had both worked on cars growing up and were comfortable fixing things. Both of them were adept with plumbing and electrical problems. Charlene's ex-husband had been a contractor, so she was educated on what was required to build a house. Connor was a jack-of-all-trades and could do pretty much anything having to do with a house.

The three of them began planning what they would need. It was not an easy task, but they were motivated and passionate about succeeding. There was never a doubt in their mind that they could do this. Their only concern was doing it right.

What would be most difficult would be to get the permits to build and getting the local government to extend power to the property. This could be overcome, but it would take some time. They decided the best way was to use a local builder with knowledge of the process. They would pay him as a consultant.

They found three possibilities, and then Charlene used dowsing and her intuition to find the best candidate. Some people think that dowsing is only used to find water, but it is a powerful technique that can tap into the mass consciousness to answer any question.

Doug, a local builder, was excited by Charlene's call and was ready to go to work. He was not very busy and could use the money. He was paid $150 per hour and was expected to work closely with the local authorities to get everything done. It was also acknowledged that they would likely use him to help build the healing center, and to find local carpenters.

They decided to build it using Archangel Michael's guidelines in the book channeled by Orpheus Phylos, titled Earth the Cosmos and You.[23] They would build twelve houses in a circular pattern. The circle would be 550 feet in diameter, with a circumference of 1728 feet. On the outer circle, the centers of each house would be 144 feet apart. This 144-foot measurement would meet Michael's requirement of increments of twelve.

In the center of the circle would be the main building and healing center. Each of the twelve houses would have a specific crystal, as stipulated by Archangel Michael, buried under the center of the house. This would create a positive energy vortex over the location. They would also use a large copper Genesa crystal in the

---

23    Earth the Cosmos and You, Virginia Essene and Orpheus Phylos, S.E.E. Publishing, 1999, p. 46.

main building. This copper crystal is a 3D representation of the flower of life and carries a strong positive energy vibration. The crystal would have enough energy to impact the entire property.

They decided against using appliances in the twelve houses on the outer circle, but to instead use the main building at the center of the circle for the kitchen area. This approach would make everyone feel like a family sharing the kitchen and food.

They would include bathrooms and showers in the outer houses, but no kitchen areas. It would be just like a hotel room. This would allow them to use small cabins that required very little plumbing. They would purchase these as ready-made and have them delivered. It was decided to purchase various sizes for different size families, from 300 square feet to 1,000 square feet in size. All would use electrical heat, and at the 7,000 feet elevation, air conditioning would not be necessary. They would use several skylights in each cabin to expose the stars at night and reduce the cost of energy to light the houses during the day. The skylights and the windows would be dual-paned to be energy efficient, and each house would use high quality insulation for energy conservation.

Because the plot of land was flat and in a meadow, it would be easy to construct the houses. They did not have to move any dirt, trees, or shrubs. All they needed to do was install cement slab foundations, along with plumbing, and begin construction. They decided to tap into the local electrical grid, while at the same time building their own. They planned to sell back to the city their surplus power. They would use two large windmills and solar panels on the roof of each house and the central building. Plus, they would rely on batteries to store their power. Once the batteries were full, they would send power back to the city's electric grid.

They planned to have their own water supply using their own wells, which they would drill. One of the reasons Charlene chose southern Colorado is that it was known to have a sufficient water table.

It was decided to first get all of their permits, septic tanks, and electrical completed before moving to Colorado. Then they would move to Pagosa Springs and work with Doug to build the central building. After they began construction on the main building, they would begin ordering a few of the prefabricated houses using their specifications.

Next, they would order and install the windmills, along with the first solar panels and storage batteries. Then they would purchase a few prefabricated greenhouses and begin growing food. Once it was all done, they would call their friends and have them join them in Colorado.

# Chapter Seven

# THE HEALING
# CENTER IS BUILT

After a few months, and with Doug's hard work, the permits were approved, along with plans to extend the power grid to their property. During this time, Charlene, Margie, and Connor meticulously planned out the center. They worked with a local architect for plans for the central building, and agreed to build a large two-story building. It was 5,000 square feet, with a dozen rooms. The healing rooms were upstairs, and downstairs was relegated to a group community living area. The largest room was downstairs and was used for both an eating area and a place for congregating. It could easily hold fifty people. There was also a large entertainment room, where people could gather to watch movies and DVDs. Another large room was designed for reading, playing games, and surfing the Internet. In many respects, it was a library room. Another large room would be used as a yoga and exercise room with an assortment of exercise equipment.

Wireless Internet was planned using a satellite connection. There were likely to be people who lived at the center who relied on the Internet for their jobs. Also, it would be used as a news source and an educational resource. Plus, it would be indispensable for shopping. As long as there were delivery companies still doing business in Pagosa Springs, you could purchase just about anything on the Internet and have it delivered.

There were no bedrooms originally planned for the central building, although some of the healing rooms could be converted into bedrooms as necessary. It was decided to purchase a few camper trailers to supplement the twelve houses. These would likely be needed as the population of the healing center grew in size. Both water and electrical hookups would be provided for the trailers. They would each be large enough to sleep at least four people. The trailer location would be outside of the circumference of the circle of houses to maintain the energy of the circle.

If they ran out of rooms, they planned to purchase more ready-made houses, or perhaps some mobile homes. They didn't want to create a mobile home park, but a few mobile homes was a possibility.

Connor wanted a screened porch on the central building, so they added a large ten- by twenty-five-foot porch in the front. It would include couches and chairs for at least twenty people. It would be a comfortable place to read or talk, especially when the weather was good.

They decided to splurge and purchase several tons of flat stones that could be used to build walkways throughout the center. These would interconnect all of the houses to the central building, as well as walkways to the trailers and parking areas. They didn't want to ostentatiously decorate or landscape the grounds. In fact, they wanted it to remain very basic and close to nature. They decided to focus on planting trees to create a beautiful setting. The extent of their decorations would be a large Native American medicine wheel and several large crystals throughout the grounds.

A large vegetable and fruit garden was planned, which included several greenhouses. The garden and greenhouses were also to be located outside of the circumference of the circle. Everyone was expected to help with food production or cooking. The garden would be a place where nearly everyone spent some time working.

One unique idea was to build a large tower as a viewing and meditation platform. This would be built out of steel and would be modeled in the shape of a double helix after a tower located in Kings Park in Perth, Australia. Connor also wanted to build a meditation labyrinth out of stones that duplicated the labyrinth at Chartres Cathedral in France.

With the architect's plans and Doug's team of carpenters, ground was broken, and they began work on the central building in early spring. Once construction began, it created a beehive of activity. Charlene, Margie, and Connor began ordering items in rapid succession. They purchased three camper trailers, one for each of them to live in while they were building the center. Then they hired a dowser to find the best place for a water well and began drilling. Once the well was completed, Connor purchased a large water tank, along with an automated pump system to keep the tank full. He then installed plumbing to provide water for the camper trailers.

There was so much to do that Connor asked if he could invite his cousin Jackson to join them. Jackson was a fantastic handyman and was also a good fit to join the center. After he came, much more work was accomplished.

Connor and Jackson began building the walkways. They also purchased a large storage building to hold all of their tools and equipment. It didn't take long for the center to begin looking like a small community.

Charlene and Margie spent a lot of time planning and ordering items to decorate the interior of the central building and the twelve houses. Most of these items would fit in the large storage building until the prefabricated houses started arriving.

After a few months and after a few of the prefabricated houses had arrived, the center looked well on its way to completion. The windmills arrived and were installed by Connor and Jackson. Then the solar panels arrived and were installed on the rooftops. Next, a watering system was installed in the three greenhouses, including some hydroponics. Charlene and Margie even had time to plant a few things in one of the greenhouses.

By the end of summer, the central building was almost finished. They were still working on the kitchen and bathrooms, but the furniture was already in place. Half of the prefabricated buildings had arrived and were installed and furnished. The other half would arrive next spring. Charlene began calling her friends and informing them that they could move in on October 1st, or they could wait until spring. It was their choice.

She sent them pictures using their wireless Internet connection and even Skyped with a few of them. Half of them chose to come in October, and the rest said they would wait until spring. They wanted to spend one last Christmas with their families and friends before making the big move to relocate and change their lives.

\* \* \* \* \*

October came, and Charlene's friends began to arrive. Everything was completed awaiting their arrival. All that was needed was for people to begin living here. By the end of October, that is exactly what they were doing. All of the houses were in use except one, as well as the three camper trailers. There were fifteen people now living at the healing center, including three families, with the rest of the people being single. Once the additional six houses were delivered and furnished, they could easily hold twenty-five people. They expected it to potentially grow into fifty people over the next few years. This would require them to purchase more prefabricated houses.

Initially, the cost would be free for those who chose to live here. However, to live here you had to be invited. And for those who came and had financial assets, it was suggested that they donate $500 a month to the community treasury. This was entirely voluntary and would help provide financing for the center. It was hoped that the members of the center would donate enough each month to make the treasury sustainable, with positive cash flow.

Once they settled in, one of the teenagers, Joey, asked if he could create a website for marketing the healing center. He had experience building websites and had time on his hands. This was quickly approved, and someone volunteered to help him. Once the website was up and running, they received several inquiries from all over the country for health issues. Charlene did not want to charge money for healing people, and wanted to provide free water and electrical hookups for people with motor homes and camper trailers. She even wanted to feed visitors for free. All the center would ask for is donations to keep the center open. This was quickly agreed. After all, with Margie's large bank account, money was currently not an issue.

Charlene, Margie, and Connor became the de facto leadership committee. They had grown close from planning and building the center, and had ideas about what they wanted. Charlene allowed two more of her close friends to be part of the leadership. They always decided things as a group, without any one person making decisions on their own.

The one overriding goal was to keep the energy of the center in the highest integrity. In many respects, reverence for the Creator was the theme. Nearly all of the adults were old-soul Gnostics, and most of them knew the truth that everything is one with the Creator. They knew that all consciousness is interconnected and interrelated, and that the source of all consciousness is God, the Creator. In essence, they knew that nothing was separate from God, and this literally meant that everything and everyone was connected to God.

These old souls had been on a spiritual path most of their adult life. They knew about reincarnation and that this lifetime, or personality, was simply a mask that was used to learn lessons and expand the awareness of the soul. They had reverence for life, and understood that they were here to help humanity and all life forms to evolve and move forward. Because love is the core of God and the core of the soul, these old souls were extremely compassionate and loving people. They knew on a very profound level that love was the pathway to God.

They were living their lives in service to God, and as a correlation, service to humanity. This is why Charlene, and the rest of the group, could not charge money to heal people. The purpose of the center was literally sacred. The center itself was considered sacred ground, much like an ancient monastery in Tibet, high in the Himalayas.

These were people who did not need any spiritual guidance from a religion or a pastor. They were beyond that. In fact, most of them were highly evolved old souls and in close contact with their higher selves and spirit guides. But more than that, they had enough wisdom to know what life was about. If someone wandered onto their property, which would happen quite often in the future, each of them could quite literally answer just about any question regarding the meaning of life, and why we are here on this planet.

The reason this enlightened group was together was because of Charlene, and her high standards. She only allowed highly aware old souls into her life. From a very early age, she knew why she was on this planet. She had come to help the planet awaken. She knew that it would be during her lifetime when the planet transformed from a planet of darkness, negativity, anger, conflict, war, etc., to one of light, love, humanity, cooperation, reverence, and unity consciousness.

What was coming in the near future was nothing less than the grand plan of God the Creator bringing humanity back to where it was nearly 100,000 years ago. To a place of spiritual awareness and profound knowing of our true selves. Back to the time of Lemuria and the early Atlantean days.

The wise old souls whom Charlene had assembled all knew why they were on the planet. They knew what was coming, and they were excited and exhilarated to be able to help during the transition. They were the midwives giving birth to the New Earth. They had some trepidation knowing that it would be chaotic in the beginning, but this was a minor inconvenience compared to their optimistic outlook for what was coming.

The countries of the world would implode as their economic, social, and cultural systems faltered. Everything would have to be reorganized and transformed into a new way of life. Our current pillage of natural resources would come to an end, and a simpler way of living would arise. Cities would be hollowed out as populations slowly evacuated to form a new life elsewhere. Perhaps the biggest changes would be in regard to spirituality. These spiritual changes would be the reason why no one wanted to go back to our old way of life. A unity consciousness would arise that very few knew was coming. It would be like the movie *Field of Dreams*, in which one man, played by Kevin Costner, and his family could see visions of baseball players on their field, but no one else could. They had to wait for everyone else to be able to see them as well.

So Charlene and her old-soul friends built the healing center, as Kevin Costner's movie character built the baseball field in the middle of his farm. Build it and they will come. That was the message Costner's character heard in the movie, and that was the message Charlene heard.

This was not a group of people who built a healing center because they wanted to heal people for a living. It was much more than that. Much more. It is difficult to describe with words what drove them and gave them passion. You can't tell someone that God exists and that they are an eternal being who is one with God, even though it is the truth. Hearing the truth is not enough. People have to experience it for themselves to know it to be true. Once this happens, they cross over from a place of faith and belief to a place of *knowing*. All of Charlene's old soul friends did not live by belief, but by *knowing*. And from this place of deep knowing, they had a degree of reverence that cannot be described with words.

This reverence allowed them to look into another soul's eyes, or even the eyes of an animal, and feel a connection to the oneness that existed between them. They knew that they were not alone, and that the journey back to a feeling of oneness was what life was all about. This knowing gave them an outlook on life that was the overriding theme of their waking moments. It provided a strong passion for giving service back to God, and as a correlation, humanity itself.

All of them could have easily lived in a monastery, and many of them had in past lives, but they didn't. They had come to help raise the vibration of the planet, and that could only happen with actions. They had come to help humanity in any way they could with the coming transition and transformation of mankind. It was a very ambitious goal, but it was literally ingrained into who they were.

Charlene had been thinking of opening a healing center since the early 1990s. She knew it would likely be a while after she got the idea. So she waited. She was so close to her spirit guides that she knew it was only a matter of time before she was given guidance to the location. Whenever she had a question, she would meditate and clear answers would come. Her relationships with her higher self and spirit guides was profound. She was spirit-led in the true sense of the term, because that is exactly how she lived her life.

When her friends began to arrive, the hugs of happiness and joy were ecstatic. It was an acknowledgment that they had succeeded in their dream, and now they could proceed with living that dream. Many people have their dreams come true, such as becoming a professional musician, artist, actor, or athlete. This is how they felt when they hugged. They had accomplished their dream.

Now they could live that dream. Every day would be a new experience of joy and excitement. They might not have been worry free, but they had achieved a sense of accomplishment and life direction that had relieved most of their stress and anxiety.

\* \* \* \* \*

Tibus was monitoring the progress at the healing center, and it was now time to make some timely additions. The first thing he wanted to add was a gifted healer. One of the teammates had found an ideal candidate and was working with Tibus to bring that person to Pagosa Springs. The problem was that the healer, Joyce, did not have a connection with any of the members of the center. Also, she was not looking for a new home and was content with her life. She lived in Santa Cruz, California and had plenty of clients to keep her busy.

Tibus decided the best way was to bring her to the center and have her look around. Once the website for the center was up and running, he had one of Joyce's friends stumble upon it while looking for new healing modalities on the Internet.

"Joyce, you have to see this." She handed Joyce her Macbook laptop.

Joyce put down the laptop and began reading. "Wow, I thought this would happen at some point. They are offering their services for free, and only request a donation to their center. They are healing as a team, which I've always been intrigued by."

"I've always wanted to see Colorado," Joyce's friend said. "Let's do a road trip and check it out."

"We can't just show up and knock on their door," Joyce said.

"It says here that they are also a teaching school. I'm sure they would allow us to visit to see if we want to be students."

"Email them and find out," Joyce said.

Her friend smiled. "Cool. This is going to be fun."

＊　＊　＊　＊　＊

The next thing Tibus needed was two people who were income earners. He found two excellent candidates. The first one was a writer who had a steady income from book sales. He was a metaphysical writer and visionary who knew that society was on the path of a major transformation. His vision fit in perfectly with the school's, and he believed that in the future, most people would end up in some form of communal living.

Tibus found a connection between a friend of the writer, Roger, and one of the members of the healing center, Jason. Tibus would first help Roger become a member using Jason's help, and then have Roger contact the writer for a visit to the healing center. Roger was a healer and was having trouble finding work and getting by financially. Bills were piling up and creating havoc, and he was looking for a way to change his life. Little did he know that Tibus was making sure that no work came his way.

Jason emailed Roger and told him about the healing center and asked him to send people to the center who needed help. Roger suddenly got an idea that he would like to work there. He inquired whether a job was available. The group decided to give the healer a chance based on Jason's recommendation. He could come and work with them for a few weeks, and if it worked out, he could stay.

After a few weeks, Roger was part of the center and a helpful addition as a healer. Shortly thereafter, he contacted the writer, who was his close friend and told him to visit. On his arrival, the writer, James, was extremely impressed with everyone at the center. He knew after one day that he wanted to live there. He wasn't a healer, but he was a writer and metaphysical teacher. He could help support the center financially, and he could give lectures. Charlene and Margie loved him. Once he asked, they immediately said yes.

\* \* \* \* \*

The second income earner was an artist. She didn't have any connection to anyone at the center, but she was a free spirit who wanted to live in a communal setting. She was frustrated with society and loathed the culture that America had become. The hyper-competitive way of life annoyed her. In many respects, she was an anarchist. She wanted a new way of life to appear, where people got along for simply being human, and where there was an abundance of love and harmony.

Her paintings sold, and she made plenty of money, but she wasn't happy. Or, I should say, she wasn't happy with the life she was forced to live. It was impossible for her to avoid the myriad of social structures that frustrated her. Everything from a dysfunctional education system, an unhealthy food industry, dumbing down television programs, the reliance on technology, Wall Street bankers running the world, and bought and sold politicians who could care less for the common man. Her heart wept at the state of affairs, but she couldn't find a way out that she so desperately wanted.

Tibus used an extreme method to get her to the healing center. He made her daughter sick. The artist loathed mainstream medicine and preferred holistic healing. She went online, forced to use a computer that she rarely used, to find help for her daughter. When she found the Pagosa Springs healing center, she decided to make the trip from Boulder, Colorado. It wasn't that far, and Tibus didn't have to nudge her much to make the trip.

Once she arrived with her daughter, she fell in love with the healing center. Everyone was so evolved and spiritually aware. The energy of the place was incredibly positive. There seemed to be a spirit of joy and love that permeated the place.

There was very little paperwork to fill out, only a single page for their contact information and the reason for the visit. The healing was a two-step process. First, they did a diagnosis using a team of healers, whoever was available. Usually, the team was at least three healers, and sometimes all of the healers at the center were present. The first thing they did during the diagnosis was to explain to the afflicted that they, the healers, could not heal them. And that they, the healers, would not be responsible for the healing. This was the reason they did not charge for the healing. They could only be facilitators and conduits in a healing that was performed in tandem with the afflicted. In other words, the person with the affliction had to be an integral part of the healing.

Some healers claim that the afflicted heal themselves. In an ideal world, that is true. But in today's world, most people have a very difficult time healing themselves. Thus, the healer or facilitator is necessary and is a very important part of the healing process. This is changing as the energy on the planet changes, however. In the future, healers will rarely be necessary. We will know how to maintain our health by keeping our energetic fields in balance. And when we do become sick, we will be able to heal ourselves. There already are several modalities available for self-healing.

For a healing to be possible, three things are necessary. First, the afflicted must *want* to be healed. Second, the afflicted needs to believe that the healing is possible. And lastly, the higher self, or soul, of the afflicted, needs to assist in the healing. If there are karmic reasons why the affliction is necessary, then the higher self will not assist.

If these three things are present, then just about any trained healer can act as a facilitator. The healer can then help move the energy, while working directly with the higher self and energy field of the afflicted. Because of this interaction between their energy fields, a healing cannot be facilitated without the consent and cooperation of the higher self. In other words, the energy fields of both the afflicted and the healer have to work together in a mutual agreement. This normally takes place beyond our conscious perception, and occurs on the quantum level.

All healings are essentially the same. They occur via a rebalancing of the energy frequencies in the body. Every cell and every organ in the body vibrates at a particular frequency. When these frequencies get out of balance, an illness manifests. While pharmaceutical drugs, surgery, radiation, magnetics, sound, color, vibration, etc., can be used to change these frequencies, it can also be done by directly manipulating the energy field of the body.

During the diagnosis, very few questions are initially asked, giving the healers a chance to connect with the integrated consciousness of All That Is. Usually, one of the healers will get a clear understanding of not only the reason the person has come, but all of the health issues present. Often these diagnoses are quite profound and explain the underlying cause of the illness. Sometimes, healers must tell the afflicted that their condition is karmic and that a healing at this time is unlikely.

After the initial diagnosis period, healers ask questions to verify what information they had picked up. Usually, a diagnosis will take less than 30 minutes, and is highly accurate. At the healing center, Charlene decided to have a notetaker present during the diagnosis. This information would be collected and added to a database using voice recognition software. This would provide a history of all of their healings. While each person is different and no two healings are identical, it was decided that this information could be valuable. It could provide a reference for how people were treated effectively and how long the healings required. For instance, how long, on average, did it take to treat hepatitis, and what modalities were the most effective?

Once the diagnosis was completed, the healers would discuss in private the best approach for the healing and which healers would work with the afflicted. Once a healer or healers began their work on the afflicted, the results varied.

Sometimes results could be noticed almost immediately, but often it would take several days, weeks, or even months for the energy field of the afflicted to change. Because the length of time for a healing was unknown, after a few healing sessions, the team of healers would perform a follow-up diagnosis to assess their progress. If it was determined that the healing would require longer than their stay, they could be worked on remotely to complete the healing.

The artist's daughter had leukemia, and it would take at least a month for a complete recovery. The artist decided to purchase a motor home and stay until it was completed. Of course, by the end of the healing she would grow too fond of the place to leave.

Chapter Eight

# THE HEALING
# CENTER OPENS

People began arriving almost immediately after the center opened. Most came for a healing, but there was also a large group of people who just wanted to see the center. They came just to look around and ask a few questions. Many of them had the idea of opening their own healing center or some type of communal living.

The website was the reason they came. Anyone who spent any amount of time searching the Internet for holistic healing probably came across the site. Their website was an ideal marketing tool, and it was practically free to maintain. They received dozens of email inquiries every day.

Charlene and Margie wanted to use the center not only for healing, but also for teaching and as an example that others could emulate. They knew that there was going to be a need for healing centers and sustainable communities throughout the country. They decided the best way to spread the word was to offer healers the ability to come and visit. Healers could stay at the center free of charge (although a donation was accepted) and work with the team of healers. It was hoped that many of these visitors would get the idea to build their own healing center.

They decided to use one of the twelve houses as a guest house for the visiting healers. The guest house had two bedrooms, and the visitors could stay for one or two weeks. Applications to visit were scrutinized by Charlene and Margie, and then applicants were put on a waiting list.

The visiting healers brought with them knowledge that could be shared with the team of healers. And the team of healers would make sure to share their knowledge with the visitors. This created a two-way transfer of knowledge that was very effective.

Most of the healing modalities involved energy work. They used the EMF Balancing Technique, Reconnective Healing, Reiki, hands-on healing, hands-off healing, sound healing, light healing, dowsing, plus several other techniques. Two of the more unique rooms at the healing center were devoted to sound and light healing. The sound room was nearly soundproof and included large crystal bowls, gongs, and a didgeridoo. The light room was a kaleidoscope of lasers that infused the body with light frequencies.

One of the rooms in the main center was used for teaching. It was here that healing knowledge was learned and shared. It was full of crystals that helped promote clear thinking. There were two cathedral crystals that were five feet tall and weighed over three hundred pounds each.

In addition to the invited visitors, who were mostly healers, many people would simply show up. One family came because of their daughter. They didn't understand her abilities and were looking for someone to help them understand. Their daughter was only nine years old, but she was a skilled psychic healer. She could see auras and heal people whenever she saw something amiss in their auric field. From the time their daughter was four, no one in their family had gotten ill. She could also see into the future and constantly predicted events that occurred. Her other skills included telepathy, which allowed her to read people's minds, and telekinesis, which enabled her to move objects with her mind.

Lizzie, the young girl, and her family were allowed to stay in the guest home for two weeks. During this time, Lizzie worked with the healing team doing both diagnosis and healing. She was such a powerful healer that sometimes she would simply walk up to the afflicted and smile and balance their energy field in a matter of seconds. However, this was not always possible for some of the afflicted. Sometimes a healing was not possible, or it could take a longer period of time.

Lizzie did not want to leave, but after two weeks, the center had to make room for new visitors who were scheduled to arrive. She was taught how to heal remotely, and it was agreed she would be emailed a list of the afflicted whom she could help. This was enough to make Lizzie accept her fate and return home. However, even at nine years old, she was determined to come back and live here.

Joyce, the healer whom Tibus had guided to the center, and her friend were accepted to live in the visitors' house for two weeks and work with the healing team. It was immediately recognized by the team that Joyce was extremely gifted, both at diagnosis and healing. She cured a man with severe hepatitis in only a few days. Then she cured a woman with cancerous tumors in a few days. Joyce was not sure if she wanted to stay, because she liked her life in Santa Cruz. However, after the two weeks were over, Charlene and Margie asked her if she would like to stay and join the center. She would be the first visitor that they had asked. Joyce was conflicted, but decided that staying and helping was the right thing to do. She loved the people and the center and what they were doing.

*　*　*　*　*

In the spring, the rest of Charlene's friends began to arrive, along with the arrival of the rest of the prefabricated houses. Soon the healing center was complete. All twelve of the houses were now furnished and occupied, along with the three trailers. Depending on how many visitors were staying in the guest house, there were approximately twenty-five people living at the center.

Some of the family members found work in Pagosa Springs to keep them busy, but most of the people stayed and lived at the center. There was plenty to do, including working in the garden and greenhouses. Also, Charlene, Margie, and Connor were always looking for volunteers to perform various jobs. The healing center took on the tone of a working business.

Once the center opened and was humming along, everyone settled into a way of life. During the day, the healers worked from 9 a.m. until 2 p.m. They worked a short day to maintain their quality of life. Some of the healers were type-A personalities and worked more hours. The rest of the group found various jobs to perform. They found that it took quite a bit of effort to maintain a community of twenty-five that was hosting both visitors and people who came for healing.

Charlene and Margie were both on the healing team, so they had to delegate much of the management of the center to Connor. He was a Ten of Spades and a Capricorn. With these personality attributes, he didn't have much difficulty keeping the center organized.

Connor was in charge of keeping supplies ordered, delivered, picked up, and paid for. He used a laptop to keep everything documented for the local bookkeeper that they hired. He also had Jackson to fix anything that broke and needed repair, which usually turned into a daily job.

Diane was in charge of the vegetable garden, fruit trees, and greenhouses and worked there nearly every day. She was given free rein to order whatever she needed, and Connor made sure it was ordered and delivered. Diane was a Jack of Diamonds and a Taurus. She was so creative that she couldn't stop with just the vegetable garden, fruit trees, and greenhouses; she had to decorate the entire healing center with trees and plants. She was always busy and worked with a smile on her face. The lettuce, spinach, kale, broccoli, tomatoes, carrots, celery, radishes, green beans, and a gamut of other vegetables kept everyone healthy and well fed.

There was always an abundance of kale, and many people used it for their daily juicing. There were a few different recipes, but the one with kale, cucumber, celery, carrot, and apple was popular.

The kitchen was managed by Karen. She had two cooks who worked for her, no pay, of course. Karen would order the food and make the daily menus. It was decided by the leaders of the center to keep the menu simple. Every day there were two or three options for breakfast, lunch, and dinner. You could not order a special meal, but had to make do with something on the menu. While most of the group were vegetarians, they did serve meat several times per week.

Because Charlene and Margie were focused on good health, they were self-educated on nutrition. The group were mostly vegans and attempted to avoid animal products (meat and dairy), processed food, GMO foods, refined sugar, high-fructose corn syrup, hydrogenated oils, and other harmful additives such as monosodium glutamate (MSG), artificial sweeteners, artificial colorings and anything you can't pronounce.

They also promoted foods that you should eat: raw fruits, nuts, and vegetables eaten daily. While eating healthy was promoted, it was recognized that a reasonable amount of unhealthy processed food would be necessary. To cook most meals, it was nearly impossible to avoid cooked and processed ingredients. It was decided to give monthly classes on nutrition to discuss healthy and unhealthy foods, as well as supplements, such as vitamins and minerals, and various superfoods.

Charlene and Margie liked to take supplements, so a host of supplements were ordered each month for the group, including multi-vitamins, fish oil capsules, colon cleanse capsules, anti-oxidant capsules, vitamin C tablets, vitamin D-3 capsules, and several others.

Some of the inhabitants used dowsing to identify which supplements they needed to take, as well as to remove any ill effects that could be caused by the food they ingested. Others liked to use prayer and meditation to purify the water using techniques discovered by Dr. Masaru Emoto.

The kitchen was open for ordering three times a day: breakfast, lunch, and dinner. If someone missed a meal, there were self-serve snacks and drinks available. There was a heated discussion to decide what would be allowed for self service snacks. They didn't want to allow sugary or artificially-sweetened drinks or high-calorie processed snacks. It was decided to provide only 100% juice drinks, along with the option of creating fresh smoothies and juices (using fruits and vegetables). For snacks, there were raw nuts (several varieties) and some whole grain crackers.

Dessert was a contentious issue. They did not want to eat well and then gain weight on high-calorie sugary desserts. It was decided to limit desserts to Saturday nights and to make them using sugar-free and non-dairy recipes. They would also provide fruit on a daily basis, which could be made into a smoothie. From experience, it was recognized that many people would eat dessert every day if it was available.

Home schooling was taught by Marisa, but also by the children themselves, based on the Anastasia series by Vladimir Megre. This series of nine books came out in Russia in the 1990s and has sold more than ten million copies. It has had a huge impact on Russia and the rest of the world. Many people believe that Vladimir invented Anastasia, but he claims she is real. She has never been photographed or interviewed, so there is no definitive proof that she exists.

The books are essentially about Anastasia, who is almost impossible to describe. She could be compared to an ascended master, such as Jesus, who has incarnated on the planet to teach us. Her abilities are similar to those of Jesus, and perhaps even more advanced in some respects. She can discuss and debate anyone on any subject, with a level of knowledge that is truly profound.

She can bilocate and move her body to another location at will. She can read your mind and react before you make an action. For this reason, she can defend herself from her enemies. I could go on and on. She is simply an amazing woman.

The Russians have a love affair with Anastasia, and most of them who have read *The Ringing Cedars* series believe she is real. Many have followed her guidelines on how to build a domain for each family. These domains are one hectare (2.5 acre) plots of land and are designed to be sustaining and self-sufficient using permaculture. The domain concept is only one of her ideas. She also explained how to educate children. Schools based on her concepts have emerged in Russia. These schools focus on allowing the children to learn as a group and literally teach each other. They learn the same subjects and material together, no matter each student's age. This has the effect of increasing learning at an exponential rate. For instance, many of the children master math at a very young age.

These Anastasia concepts were used at the healing center. Thus, Marisa would allow the children to set up their own curriculum and learn together. There was no such thing as first grade, second grade, or any grade levels at all. Instead, everyone learned the same subject, and children were considered equals. This had the effect of giving children extraordinary self-confidence and a thirst for knowledge. Young children were learning subjects that were normally not taught until they were teenagers. There were no limitations on what could be learned. The children got to choose what they wanted to learn. Then they pursued that subject until it was decided to move on to another.

The school was open from 8 a.m. until 2 p.m., and was closed on Friday, Saturday, and Sunday. Again, hours were restricted to create a quality of life. There was no burden placed on the children. They were free to do homework in the afternoons. They were also given July and August off for summer holiday.

The school room had a large main screen that was used for several different things. Each student had a laptop that could be shared on the main screen. Also, they could surf the Internet as a class looking for information. Often students or Marisa would share their screen with the rest of the class. The main screen was a focal point of their learning. Sometimes they would use a camera and communicate with another school. They communicated with three other schools who used similar teaching methods (all based in Russia) who liked to share about once a month. All of the students got to know each other by speaking English, which the Russian students spoke fairly well. And many of the students at the healing center were learning Russian.

These sharing sessions between schools was amazing. The students would present what they were learning and share knowledge. The Russians were learning architecture in order to build a new classroom. The American children at the healing center wanted to do the same. The problem was that the Russian school had about sixty students of all ages from five to eighteen. However, the Pagosa Springs healing center only had six children. Not quite enough to master architecture and build a school room. But they still wanted to study it, and they did.

The Russians were interested in energy healing and were excited when Joyce gave a session on the subject. They also liked it when James, the writer, gave a lecture on the Science of the Cards and Numerology. Anything that the children found interesting was studied as a group. The information that was gathered by the children was collected and stored in Evernote, an Internet data collection application. Then this information could be searched and read in the future by the students. And because it was an Internet-based application, they could share it with other schools.

There were no tests and no grading, and children could literally learn what they wanted. The only required subjects were reading, writing, and math. These were considered the foundation that all students should learn. Everything else was left up to the students; they could decide how much effort to apply to a subject. Marisa thought that public speaking was beneficial to the student's self-esteem. So, she had the children give several presentations to the class each year, as well as speak in front of the class nearly every week on a short topic or question.

Because reading, writing, and math were emphasized, there was an abundance of assignments on these core subjects. The students didn't mind because they knew it was only done so that they would get better, and that these assignments were only for practice. There was no pressure to compete with the other students.

\* \* \* \* \*

During the first year, the healing center had become a well-organized operation. They healed many people who came with severe afflictions, and the people who lived at the center truly enjoyed their new home. Everyone came to know each other as family, and a camaraderie had developed. It was an incredibly harmonious environment, even with ill people constantly arriving. Most of the afflicted were healed during their visit, and those who were not, either required more time using remote healing or could not be healed due to their karma – past life or other soul issues.

Visitors and the afflicted were greeted with genuine smiles and warm-hearted acceptance when they arrived. Nearly everyone who stepped foot on the grounds of the healing center found it to be one of the most humane places on the planet. It felt like sacred ground, due to the beauty of the place and the atmosphere of service to humanity. It was a magical place where people were cured of serious afflictions without any drugs or side effects.

\* \* \* \* \*

After the first year that the center was open, the world experienced a traumatic life-changing event. In the U.S., it was comparable to 9-11, only this time everyone knew we would not recover. Our way of life was lost and there would be no going back. The event that shook the world was the U.S. Government implementing a currency reset. A new currency was issued that devalued the dollar by thirty percent. This had the impact of creating instant inflation and effectively defaulting on thirty percent of the debt.

Old dollars had to be exchanged for new dollars. Whereas the new dollars were worth thirty percent less than old dollars, those who owed debt, such as a mortgage or a corporate loan, now owed thirty percent less. Thus, the U.S. Government instantly owed thirty percent less in debt. On the other hand, citizens with savings now had thirty percent less wealth.

The fallout caused the world to become enveloped in one economic crisis after another. And because the global economy was so tightly integrated, it was impossible for the U.S. not to be severely impacted. Whereas during the 2008 economic crisis, the dollar strengthened versus other currencies, this time, the opposite occurred. The dollar crashed as countries such as China and Japan sold their U.S. Treasury bonds. The world financial system witnessed an epic change of historical proportions.

As the dollar crashed, investors pulled their money out of American assets, such as the dollar, stocks, and bonds. This caused a liquidity problem, and then the banking system and stock markets crashed. Without a viable financial system, many companies and corporations became bankrupt in a matter of weeks. Trillions of dollars in assets were lost as stock and bond values collapsed.

Within months of these events, the unemployment rate skyrocketed to heights no one expected. Suddenly there were no jobs, and local, state, and federal governments were left with much less money to fund the programs that so many people depended upon.

After these events unfolded, the healing center was inundated with visitors who wanted a place to live. A tent city was built by squatters who just wanted to be near what was perceived as the future way of life. These people constantly loitered on the healing center grounds and disrupted what had become a beautiful place to live. The tranquility that had existed was interrupted and impinged.

Charlene would not allow any guns at the healing center, nor any form of security. This made it difficult to control the squatters. At first, they called the local police to report trespass violations, but the authorities only came once or twice, and then stopped due to funding constraints and higher priorities. Their attitude was that since you live in the country, take care of yourself.

Finally, it was decided that their only option was to purchase more land and increase the size of the healing center. In the near term, there would be no more tranquil wonderland that they initially built, but they would do the best they could to accommodate as many people as possible.

They purchased another fifty acres next door to the center and built a small community. It was hoped that this new community would take squatters away from the healing center and become the focus of the wanderers who continued to arrive.

Charlene and Margie decided to take a sabbatical from being part of the healing team and build the new community. They built it similarly to the healing center, although it did not have the twelve houses in a circular pattern. Instead, it had a large central building, which was used for eating and congregating. Then they created several rows of sleeping cabins. It was basically a very efficient small community where people could live together and share everything. They built a large vegetable garden and installed greenhouses, along with a park for children and a dog run.

Instead of purchasing prefabricated buildings, Charlene decided to have Doug build them using help from the squatters living in the tent city. If they built their own community, then they would have a strong sense of pride. She also hoped that if they were given a community that they would protect the healing center and honor its mission to heal people in a tranquil environment.

While the healing center was not built specifically for communal living, the new community was built exactly for that purpose. The members of this community were industrious and motivated to create a sustainable community. They used the Internet, which Connor and Jackson installed, to market various products that people in the community had created. Before long, the new community was actually cash-flow positive.

What started out as a somewhat hostile group of squatters, became a model community for others to emulate. It didn't take long for news of these two novel communities to reach the masses. There were many reporters and camera crews who made their way to Pagosa Springs to interview Charlene and Margie. They quickly became celebrities. The medical and pharmaceutical industries tried to tarnish the healing center as a group of untrained, non-licensed, quacks. However, stories were leaking out about the myriad of miracles that were occurring at the center and their high success rate at treating severe afflictions. As the mainstream healthcare system continued to falter due to severe budget cuts from financial woes, the medical industry was losing the battle of public opinion.

The world was changing and changing dramatically. Waiting for our old way of life to return was looking more and more like the wrong choice. Instead, people were ready for something new, even if that meant a complete break from the past. When they heard about this new unorthodox healing center, and the new community built next to it that was cash-flow positive, it was the type of hope they wanted to hear. Everyone was looking for something positive that could be replicated. Americans were used to following the herd or following the trend, and this was something they could follow.

Of course, not everyone accepted this new way of life. In fact, it was still only a small minority who were interested. But word was getting out, and they were changing the hearts and minds of more people every day. The idea of living in a sustainable manner had a broad-based appeal. The thought of a small community feeding itself, employing itself, powering itself, and healing itself, was considered a panacea to a large number of people.

The next event that kicked started the move to communal living was when Texas seceded to become an independent country. This historic event changed the attitudes of many people regarding the future direction of America. Texas seceded for one simple reason: they were tired of the federal government telling them how to live. If they were going to let the federal government have such a large impact on the quality of their lives, then they wanted more in return. Finally, they said enough and voted for secession.

After Texas seceded, many states became more amenable to allowing communal living to prosper. States realized that these self-supporting communities would take pressure off government programs. Moreover, secession was a call for less government and more libertarian attitudes of allowing people to make their own choices on how they wanted to live.

Once Texas seceded, there was a wave of new communities built across America. They were nearly all based on the concept of community sharing and sustainability. Many of these communities had their own group of energy healers. What Charlene and Margie had started had now become common. Slowly and steadily people were evacuating the large cities and forming much smaller communities in the countryside. Nearly all of these new communities were less than 1,000 people, and most were smaller than 200 people.

# Chapter Nine

# THE U.S. CHANGES

The Pagosa Springs healing center was the beginning of a huge wave of migration from the cities to the countryside. Small communities began to appear throughout the country, although it was much more apparent in the West, where alternative lifestyles were faster to catch on.

Nearly all of these communities were based on the concept of sharing and humanity. In other words, all of the members of the community were considered family and taken care of equally. There was no racism or discrimination, although there was still a hodgepodge of belief systems that created a degree of conflict.

In the new-age communities, such as the Pagosa Springs healing center, Gnostic spirituality thrived. The definition of a Gnostic is simple: a direct connection to God. Gnosis means knowledge, and a Gnostic has direct knowledge of God. A true Gnostic lives by knowing and not by faith. Thus, a Gnostic does not get his or her beliefs from a doctrine or a book. Instead, their beliefs come from within and from experience. A Gnostic develops their own belief system and follows their own spiritual path. There are no formal churches or ministers for this group, although it is not uncommon for some to attend a local Christian or Unitarian Church.

At the Pagosa Springs healing center, which was similar to many of the new-age communities that were sprouting, spirituality was a personal affair. There were those who shared their beliefs openly, but it was not expected for anyone to follow a doctrine or set of beliefs. Members of the community next door to the healing center would come over for regularly scheduled spiritual lectures.

These were given both inside the main building and sometimes outside out in nature's beauty.

* * * * *

Charlene stood in the large dining room in front of a group of people who had come to hear her speak. Nearly half of the healing center members and another dozen from the next door community were present. It was a Saturday afternoon, and they would have a dinner party after her lecture.

It was one of their educational lectures, where anyone could be a presenter. All you needed to do was schedule an event and post it on the bulletin board in the center's office. The office's main task was to admit visitors, but it was also used for several other duties. Much of the center's business was done there, along with all of the record keeping. It held the main phone, which needed to be monitored during the day. Usually, someone worked at the office every day from 8 a.m. until 3 p.m. They also monitored the center's email account and received packages from delivery companies.

Charlene did not have a microphone, because there were only twenty-five people, and they could all sit close to the front. When the room filled up, they had a PA system with a microphone that was used.

"Thank you for coming," Charlene began. "Tonight, I want to talk about the coming wave of Gnostic spirituality and what it all means. These are my beliefs and opinions, so do not take them as gospel.

"From my perspective, I believe that the world's religions are steadily becoming less relevant. For instance, no longer does everyone believe that we are separate from each other, or separate from God the Creator. This is not something you will hear at your local church.

"Many have begun to recognize that we are all interrelated and connected to one consciousness. This singularity is beginning to change our way of life and our way of perception. No longer does everyone think of themselves as separate individuals. That concept is losing its relevance. Instead, as a society, we are beginning to recognize our connection to one another, and our connection to the Creator.

"The awareness of this connection leads us to be of service to humanity and to the Creator. It literally changes our perceptions and motives. No longer do we think in terms of service to self. Instead, we think in terms of service to others, and service to humanity.

"This subtle change is starting to change the world in a very positive way. By thinking in terms of the group, instead of the self, the ego becomes marginalized. Of course, the ego is a formidable foe and isn't easily vanquished."

Charlene walked over to a large screen and clicked a button on a remote device. The screen then displayed the following:

- Envy
- Gluttony
- Greed
- Lust
- Pride
- Sloth
- Wrath

"The only sin, really, is pride, because all of the others stem from pride. Pride is the opposite of service to humanity and service to the Creator, which is our ultimate goal. Pride is selfishness and feeling puffy about ourselves. Pride is the ultimate ego trait. It is how the ego traps us into thinking we are separate from God."

"Is that really possible to remove the seven deadly sins from our lives?" asked someone from the audience.

"Perhaps not completely," Charlene replied, "but we can marginalize them to a large extent. It is our goal as Gnostics to get as close to spirit as possible. For this to happen, we need to exude integrity, virtue, and gratitude. Those three words are the core of our true self, along with love. I have found that by living a life of integrity, virtue, and gratitude, the seven deadly sins are mostly marginalized."

"How do you do it?" someone asked.

"For me," Charlene said, "the key is combining being kind, calm, and compassionate, with integrity, virtue, and gratitude. The first part is living with unconditional love, and the second part with the highest moral values. The final piece is staying grounded, centered, and connected to my soul. I find myself living one foot in this dimension of reality and one foot in the spiritual dimension, connected to my soul."

A young girl raised her hand.

Charlene pointed to the girl. "Yes?"

"How do you stay connect to your soul?" she asked.

Charlene hesitated. "That's a difficult question to answer. How we each find and connect to our soul requires an individual experience, or series of experiences that lead to that outcome. In other words, I can't tell you with words because it happens to each of us in a different manner. What I do know is that you must experience your soul to know it.

"There are teachers, seminars, and books that can lead you to experience your soul, but there is not a single way that everyone can follow. If it were that easy, then there would be a bestselling book called *How to Experience Your Soul*. Alas, such a book does not exist.

"So, there are no prescribed steps that everyone can follow to experience their soul. Most people who have experienced their soul were awakened directly by their higher self or spirit guides. That is how it happened to me. One of my spirit guides decided to make his presence known. Once that happened, it was only a matter of time before my consciousness became keenly aware of the interaction that occurs between my waking consciousness and an internal intelligence that is not of this world.

"For instance, I am constantly guided while living my daily mundane life. Sometimes I call these interventions quinky dinks. I know from experience that these subtle interventions by my guides or higher self are too timely and helpful to be mere coincidence. This is especially true when they happen as a series of random events that are all closely related, leading to a specific outcome.

"I could give you several examples, but I will give you one that happened yesterday. I told the universe that I was looking for someone who was a Club card to help me in the office because those who are Clubs tend to be very smart. Shortly after, Jane came into the office and asked if we needed help. I asked her what day she was born, and she is a 2 of Clubs, born on May 30."[24]

Several people in the room laughed.

"Now, a skeptic would say this was just a coincidence. However, I know from experience that this happens to me all the time. It is these experiences that reveal to me that the spirit world exists. These experiences have become so real that my conviction about the spirit world has transformed from belief to knowing. A skeptic would say that *knowing* the spirit world exists is impossible. But I contend that my knowing that I exist as a soul is just as genuine to me as their belief that they exist as a human being."

---

24    1 = Ace of Hearts, 13 = King of Hearts, 14 = Ace of Clubs, 26 = King of Clubs, 27 = Ace of Diamonds, 39 = King of Diamonds, 40 = Ace of Spades, 52 = King of Spades. To calculate your card, multiply your month x 2, add the day, then subtract from 55. For instance, my birthday is March 18th. 3 x 2 = 6 + 18 = 24. 55 – 24 = 31. 31 = 5 of Diamonds.

Charlene paused and looked at the girl. "There is a short-cut to finding your soul, and that is to have a paranormal experience in which you communicate with the other side. This often occurs when people have near-death experiences. When people survive these experiences, they often come back without a fear of death, along with an overwhelming belief that their soul exists.

"Many children today are having paranormal experiences without a near-death experience. This is due to their advanced spiritual development. These are evolved old souls who have come to save the planet and the human race.

"If you don't have a paranormal experience, you can still attempt to find your soul. However, this is hard work and requires a spiritual path. Which path you choose is up to you and can include a gamut of spiritual practices. Some people try nearly everything on their quest, and not everyone is successful. But know that the soul is there to be found."

Another hand went up, and Charlene pointed at the individual.

"Isn't the veil thinning between this dimension and the spiritual dimensions, and making it easier for people to find their soul?"

Charlene nodded. "Definitely. The vibration of the planet is increasing, thereby making us more spiritual and lighter in density. There are children today who can do remote telepathy. In other words, they can have communications with other children remotely, even across the world thousands of miles away. I don't know of any adults who can do this yet, but the children's DNA is changing more rapidly. The combination of their new DNA and the higher vibration of the planet makes this possible.

"Over the last fifty years, people have spent years and even decades trying to find their soul. I think that today it can happen much more quickly. In fact, I think that nearly any individual who makes a significant effort can find their soul. We are entering an era where the soul will be so tangible that almost everyone will recognize that it is real."

Another person raised their hand. "Are you saying that if we marginalize our ego, it is possible that we will experience our soul?"

Charlene smiled. "Yes, that is what I am saying. When you consciously try to marginalize the ego in your daily life by keeping your mind quiet, the soul will help you. In fact, the soul will be so excited that you are trying to find it, that it will do everything it can to prove to you that it is real.

"For instance, it is not easy to marginalize a busy mind, which is how the ego controls you. Often, the ego reveals itself using fear. We know fear comes from the ego because fear and the truth cannot coexist. Why? Because once you know the truth, fear is eliminated. The soul, the higher self, is unlimited. It cannot contain fear.

"So, how do you eliminate fear? That is not easy. Fear arises because people are afraid that their life or way of life is going to be taken away or become more difficult. Thus, if you look at fear deeply, you will see that it actually manifests from arrogance or selfishness, which is the sin of pride. People believe that their life is more important to them than service to God. In fact, people are confused, or more precisely, they are unaware of the truth. They see themselves as the center of their own existence, and anything that threatens that existence manifests as fear. In other words, fear manifests from a lack of knowledge of the soul. Anyone who attempts to marginalize fear by quieting their busy mind, will eventually uncover the soul."

"Why does the soul become exposed?" someone asked.

"Because a connection to the soul is the pathway to the truth and what we are all seeking. The soul is waiting for us to call on it, to find it," Charlene replied. "There is a saying that you either live by fear or by love. And because the soul is love, when you live by love, you are living by the soul. The more you live by love, the closer you get to your soul, and it will make its presence known."

Charlene paused, and then added, "Once you find the soul and begin living by it, fear will evaporate from your life and be replaced by love and trust."

"Completely?" the same person asked.

Charlene sighed. "Unfortunately, not for most of us, but it is something we can strive for. We are human, so fear is going to remain to a certain extent. This is also true for anger. It is nearly impossible to completely eliminate fear or anger. However, we can marginalize both to a large extent, so that they are barely a hindrance in our life. And when they do appear, we will see them for what they are, the ego pushing our buttons."

"I think I understand what you are saying now," the same person said. "The ego is blocking the soul and doing everything that it can to hide it from us. Once we proactively marginalize the ego, then the soul will reveal itself to have been there all along, thereby revealing the truth."

Charlene smiled. "Brownie points for you. Just remember, when you have marginalized your ego to such an extent that you are now living your life through love and trust, the knowledge of the soul will be impossible to deny.

"Thus, if you live your life on a spiritual path and follow a spiritual lifestyle, the soul will expose itself. I can't tell you when or how, but at some point, the soul will make its appearance. It will let itself be known. When this happens, you will have an epiphany and will cross over from living by belief to living by knowing. It will be an OMG moment where you realize that you have lived more than just this lifetime, much more. You will *know* that you are an eternal soul."

Charlene paused. "That's enough thinking for one night. I think it's time to eat. Anyone hungry?"

\* \* \* \* \*

The next door community was integrating with the healing center in a very positive way. They were incorporating many of the same ways of living, such as using a communal kitchen where everyone ate together. They even supported Gnostic beliefs, such as reincarnation and the oneness of humanity. There were many Christians, but they did not demand to follow Christian beliefs and customs, such as Lent and Easter.

The concept of equality and sharing was strong in the new community. Everyone was treated as an equal, and there was very little squabbling about how people should live and think. Nearly everyone spent some time growing or harvesting food. This was expected and became a way of life. Giving back and being grateful for the opportunity to live here was respected.

The new community sold many of their extra fruit and vegetables at the farmers market in Pagosa Springs. The market became so successful that people came from miles around to buy fresh fruit and vegetables, and they even shipped some of their vegetables to nearby towns. The quality of the food was excellent, and of course was organic.

Whereas the healing center was demure and reverent, the new door community was more bombastic and celebrated life. Every Saturday night they had a community barbeque that nearly everyone attended. It was always a lively affair, with a lot of loud noise from boisterous talking. Some of the members imbibed in alcohol, but the reverence exhibited next door at the healing center had the effect of limiting excess and public drunkenness.

Sometimes the members would perform music and turn it into a free concert. These ad-hoc concerts were actually quite good and created a high degree of ebullience and joy. There was very little gloominess or feelings of melancholy that their old way of life was lost and not coming back. In many respects, the people who lived here were happier now than when they were living in cities and towns. They didn't have the same creature comforts that they were used to, but what they had now was a sense of community. They no longer felt like they were on their own, and at the mercy of corporations and government. Here, they not only felt free, but secure and safe.

Whereas the residents of the healing center did not carry weapons or allow guns on their grounds, the new community was quite comfortable defending their land and homes. Anyone who came around who was not wanted, was quickly made aware that they could either leave or else their safety could not be guaranteed. Charlene and the other healing center members were not comfortable with this method, but they decided from the beginning that it would be up to the new community members to make their own rules.

The only thing Charlene and the other healing center members could do was set an example and hope that it would have a positive impact. In many respects, this was working. The new community was actually a highly moral, compassionate group. In fact, a small percentage of this new community were Gnostics, with beliefs quite similar to those of the healing center.

Perhaps the biggest difference between the communities was their diet. Those living in the healing center tended to be mostly vegetarians with very little red meat consumption and a desire to eat more fresh foods. The next door community was not ready to go vegetarian and ate more meat, dairy products, and processed foods. The rules on dessert that were used by the healing center definitely did not apply next door. In fact, they had become connoisseurs of homemade ice cream and a wide variety of pastries. Eating healthy was not ignored, but it was not a priority either. They tended to focus on enjoying life, and the move toward spirituality and living a sacred life was slow in coming.

\* \* \* \* \*

The young kids and adolescents at the new community had a strong desire to investigate what was happening next door at the healing center. They were curious about energy healing and the spirituality of the members next door. Something interesting was happening, and they wanted to know about it.

At first they would just come over in small groups and snoop around asking questions. Then they eventually began attending classes on spirituality that were offered by Charlene and James, the writer. These classes were also attended by some of the adults of the healing center.

The first time James taught the children from the next door community, it was a bit of a scandal. The children went home and told their parents what James said. Some of the parents were not happy and stormed over to complain. They were told that James taught the truth and that they should attend one of his classes to find out for themselves what he was teaching. The parents who accepted this explanation decided to attend the following week. When they appeared, James decided to give the same lecture.

"Good evening, everyone, and thanks for coming," James opened, with kind hearted remarks.

Everyone was gathered in the large dining room because the number was greater than twenty, which was about the maximum size for the teaching room.

"For those of you who came last week, this might be a little bit boring, but I am going to repeat what I said last week for the newcomers who I see tonight. Starting next week, we will begin progressing with new ideas.

"Let me begin by describing how life works, and then I will give an in-depth explanation for the meaning of life. This plane of reality is called the third dimension. It is a physical reality, although that physicality is an illusion. In actuality, all matter is vibrating energy, with a core of consciousness. This consciousness is alive and integrated into a unity consciousness that makes up the whole.

"This unity consciousness includes both conscious beings and animals, as well as all inanimate objects and even the air that we breathe. All is conscious, and all is alive, even if it appears to be dead. A burnt tree is alive. A dead animal is alive. A rock is alive. They are alive because nothing cannot be conscious.

"The entirety of this unity consciousness can be thought of as God, the Creator. The whole exists as a oneness that encompasses all of existence. This can be thought of as a matrix of consciousness that interrelates and connects everything. When I say everything, I'm not just talking about life forms, such as humans, plants, and animals. I mean literally everything, from the ground that you walk on, to the air that you breathe. It is all alive and conscious.

"When you throw a rock and it lands on a plant, they both can "feel" the event. In fact, both of them have emotions and can react with fear and apprehension. If they were connected to a device that could record their reactions, you would be amazed to find out that they are alive.

"How can this be? Well, the planet itself is alive, and all aspects of it. And as humans, it is our responsibility to respect this life, because we are literally one with it. Why? Because the source of our consciousness, and the source of consciousness of the planet is the same. We all originate from the same place. We all connect to the Creator.

"Note that I did not use the word originated, which is past tense. The source of our consciousness is very real, and it does not originate in this plane of existence. Where we are from, and the core of our existence, comes from the Creator itself.

"In other words, our bodies are not self-contained. The consciousness that gives us life and animation does not originate within our bodies. The source of our consciousness comes from the same place, the Creator. This is how and why we are all one consciousness, and why there is no separation between us. This is also how telepathy works."

James paused and scanned the audience. Some of the adults from the next door community were glassy-eyed and didn't know what to think. Many were skeptical that he didn't know what he was talking about. The children, on the other hand, were fascinated and listening intently.

"Okay, let's continue. The planet and life forms were created by us and the Creator as the ultimate expression of creativity. In fact, me and you, and other souls, are constantly creating new worlds and new universes. We are very creative and we never stop creating. When we create a universe or solar system with planets, we like to experience them. We do this so that our souls can grow and evolve. Essentially, we turn these planets into schools.

"Quite likely, everyone in this room has incarnated over a hundred times, and perhaps much more. Myself, I have incarnated more than 1,000 times. Why do we do this? Again, for the evolvement and growth of the soul. The Creator, or God, is perfect and complete, and does not require evolvement, for perfection cannot be improved upon. However, for the sake of creativity, the Creator spawns sparks of energy that manifest as souls. These souls, of which we are each one, have the potential to become god-like. In fact, we are each gods in the making.

"Each of us has the potential to evolve to become extraordinary souls. However, we do not exist as separate individuals, apart from God. In other words, we don't have a true individual identity. We can't, because we are one with each other, and one with the Creator. Our separateness and individuality is an illusion. This does not mean that we do not exist, for indeed we do. This may seem like a paradox, but the closer you get to a paradox, the closer you get to the truth.

"Now we come to the meaning of life. The meaning of life, is life itself. Notice how this resembles a paradox, and when you find a paradox you are close to the truth. Because our individuality is an illusion, you cannot say that the meaning of life is for the soul to evolve. However, our evolvement is quite real and one of the reasons we are here. God the Creator is beyond our understanding, and when we try to assign meaning to our individual lives, we end up trying to understand God, which is impossible. Again, another paradox."

Several of the young adolescents smiled at God's complexity.

"So, we don't exist as individuals, yet as individual souls we spend lifetime after lifetime evolving. Thus, we learn as individuals even though we don't exist as individuals. Eventually, we come to understand, or become aware, that we are all one consciousness and literally one with our source, the Creator. However, this process is very long and no one in this room has attained this level of awareness. I am close, and perhaps so are many of you, but if we truly had this awareness we would be ascended masters, and no longer need to incarnate.

"I opened this lecture by describing this level of reality as the third dimension. This is the physical plane of existence. There are several other dimensions which are non-physical spiritual planes. These are where souls exist as discarnate light beings. We spend much more of our lives as light beings in the spiritual dimensions than on the physical plane of the third dimension. Living as a light being is truly home, and the physical world of the third dimension is a temporary reality that is used for the growth of the soul.

"There are also 4th and 5th dimensional quasi-physical planets. In fact, Earth is in the process of evolving into one of these types of planets. These are used for advanced souls who have outgrown the limitations of the third dimension, but still desire to incarnate into a somewhat constricted environment. Arcturus and the Pleiades star systems have 5th dimensional planets. The Arcturians and Pleiadians are currently helping Earth to evolve into a 5th dimensional planet.

"Currently on Earth, there are many advanced souls who would normally not incarnate to the physical third dimension. They are here because Earth is going through a profound transition into a higher vibration, the 4th and 5th dimensions. There was literally a calling that went out to the universes that Earth needed volunteers for a pivotal time of change. This calling was of the highest priority because the outcome will literally impact all of the universes. It is critical that Earth's civilization does not destroy itself, but instead becomes a planet of higher vibration."

James paused. "I'm getting ahead of myself. I need to explain more about reincarnation and how life works. Each of us is on a very long journey of evolving our soul. The way this journey works is that we do a lot of planning and have a lot of help. The planning occurs when we are in between incarnations on the spiritual planes. We each belong to a soul group who generally incarnates together. This is why the people in your life often seem so familiar to you, and you feel a strong affinity.

"Soul groups and individual souls often plan their lives together. However, it is a quite complex process. Each soul has its own agenda for growth and they have to correlate their lives with the agendas of other souls. Also, each lifetime will impact future lifetimes. This is commonly called karma. So, when you exit from this lifetime you will get back together with your soul group and review each of your lives. You will analyze where you are each at from a spiritual perspective and get an understanding of what you need to learn next. Again, this is often done as a group. If one person is stuck, the group will work together to help that person evolve.

"In addition to your own analysis of what you need to do next to evolve your soul, you also have highly evolved spirit guides who help. They will give you a list of potential lives that you can live next. Quite often they will give you three options. If you do not like any of these options, you can have more options. For this lifetime, it took me twenty-seven options before I found the right fit."

"How do you know that?" someone asked.

"I had a reading from a medium that was profoundly accurate. There is no reason for me to doubt it. However, the reason it took so many options is because my soul group did not want to incarnate at this time. They knew it would be a difficult period and decided against it. Also, I am a 5th-level old soul priest, and it was hard to find a family that wanted to live with a real priest. I'm not only a real priest, but a highly evolved priest. Any family who took me was going to be confronted with deep spiritual issues that I would expose.

"Anyway, we spend a great deal of time planning on the other side, the spiritual dimensions, when we are not incarnate. We know who our parents are going to be, our personality traits, our intelligence level, our susceptibility to illness, who we are likely to marry, and on and on. No one is born without being prepared for the possible experiences they will have. In fact, life is perfect without any accidents for this reason. Planning is so intricate, that even the day we are born is planned in advance. It is chosen for the personality traits that we need to accomplish our goals.

"We all come into this life with an understanding of who we will be and what our lives will be like. There are various potential outcomes for these lives, where we get to choose the direction at certain points in our life. This is where free will comes into play. However, most of our free will decisions are made prior to our incarnation. For instance, we decide before we are born whether we are going to be a doctor, a politician or someone famous. In fact, it is amazing to what detail we make decisions prior to our incarnation.

"There is such a thing called agreements, and many souls agree to help each other when they incarnate during the same time frame. This is why we feel compelled to help others or even sometimes hurt others. Souls work together to help each other learn lessons so that we can move on.

"Nearly all souls are here to evolve. They do that by experiencing lessons that they need to learn in order to advance. Some souls who are on Earth at this time are so highly evolved that they are only here to help humanity. They cannot acquire any karma, nor do they need to learn anything. They have already evolved to the point where they are learning from a place of complete freedom. However, for the rest of us, we need to obtain that level of freedom. Once it is achieved, you can choose to create in any manner that you desire. It is this ultimate freedom that we desire, and the reason why we strive to evolve the soul.

"This level of freedom is restricted by the Creator, because we can create quite a mess without a high degree of spiritual awareness and maturity. In many respects, we are isolated from those who have achieved this level of awareness. This is the reason why when we exit this life we will return to our soul group. And this is why it is important that we accomplish our goals and increase our level of spiritual awareness during this lifetime.

"Thus, we arrive at another paradox, and again, unless you are constantly running into paradoxes, you have not gotten close to God. The paradox is that even though we are eternal souls and our core is unconditional love and everlasting joy, our lives are quite serious. To make this paradox even more baffling, the best way to live is to not take our lives too seriously, but to relax and live with very little anxiety. Yet, at the same time, we have a strong desire to achieve our soul lessons so that we can evolve towards enlightenment. The Creator is basically saying to be serious about accomplishing our goals, but not to live too seriously."

James grinned. "I think I have covered the basics of how life works. Are there any questions?"

"I think I understand," someone replied. "The goal of the soul is to evolve and become god-like, and this can only happen through experience. So, we go on this long spiritual journey of incarnations slowly becoming more aware of who we truly are, which is connected to God. And after we climb this tall mountain of difficulty we are rewarded with the freedom to live and create what we want as ascended masters."

James nodded. "Yes, that's pretty much how it works. It's another paradox, because what we are really doing with our experiences is remembering. In other words, it appears that we are learning lessons, when it fact we are simply remembering who we are, and what we can do.

"For instance, Jesus was no different than us from a soul perspective. Souls are souls, and we are basically all the same. What made him appear to be different was his level of awareness. However, we all have the same potential that he manifested. In fact, there are many children today who possess many of his abilities."

"What do you mean?" asked one of the adolescents.

James smiled. "I'm glad you asked. Many of the children born today, and over the last couple of decades, can be called children of light. These souls are highly evolved and many of them possess extraordinary abilities, such as telepathy, telekinesis, clairvoyance, clairaudience and other abilities. Some of them are healers of Jesus' level. They can instantly view the human energy field and know if there is an imbalance. Then they can restore most imbalances using an infusion of energy.

"These gifts are only a small part of the reason why these children of light have been arriving. They are here to raise the vibration and consciousness of the planet. Even more than that, they are here to lead us. They are wise old souls and very strong. They will show us the way forward. Especially, when it comes to spirituality, human interaction, and reverence for the planet and all of her life forms.

"Perhaps the greatest gift they will give us is the understanding that truth and spirituality is an individual experience, and not a group experience. Thus, they will usher in the end of organized religion. They will show us that God is unknowable and thus the truth is unknowable. All of us must find the truth for ourselves, which is our personal truth about life. We can share our truths, but they must be our own. We can't borrow someone else's truth to become enlightened."

"I like that!" replied one of the adolescents. "No one can tell me what to believe."

"More than that," James said, "you are free to find your own beliefs."

James paused. "Do you see the ramifications? No longer will judgment be pervasive. Now people will be allowed to believe whatever they want and be accepted for those beliefs. Their beliefs will be perceived as their own personal truth."

One of the adolescents clapped their hands. "Oh, this is good! You mean politicians and preachers will finally stop telling us how to live our lives?"

James nodded. "I think so. I think that is where these children of light will lead us. We are each going to be free to live our lives as we see fit without anyone judging our choices. Of course, this won't happen this year or next, but this type of spiritual awareness is coming soon."

"You're talking about utopia," one of the adults from next door said.

"Yes," James said, "or at least a semblance of utopia. That is where we are headed. No longer will the world be based on competition and conflict, and who has the most money. Instead, the world is going to be based on love and trust. This will manifest as the world steadily becomes aware of oneness and a unity consciousness."

"Unity consciousness?" asked the same adult, in a skeptical voice.

"Yes," James said, "that is exactly where we are headed. I don't say this as conjecture or a belief. Indeed, the recognition of unity consciousness is the destiny of this planet. And the time for it to begin to unfold is during our lifetime."

James stopped. The children were smiling and the adults were skeptical. It sounded like new-age propaganda to most of them.

"Can you explain this unity consciousness?" the same adult asked.

"I can try," James replied. "The planet is going to return to 4th and 5th dimensional reality. This will allow people to connect directly to the source of their consciousness – their soul – and directly with each other. People are already doing this today. It will just become common in the future and as normal as breathing.

"A direct link with each other is basically the definition of unity consciousness. In the near future, society will no longer relate to each other as distinct individuals, but instead will see each other as connected in some way. Initially, and this is already happening, people will feel a close affinity with others. This affinity will increase in degree as the crystalline grid strengthens. As people become more in tune and aware of the link between the physical plane (their body) and spiritual plane (their soul, guides, and higher self), they will recognize the connection they have with others.

"Thus, unity consciousness initially will begin from the multitudes of people who are spiritually aware. Steadily, they will become conscious of their connection with others, and to humanity. Then this awareness will progress to the point where everyone transcends 3rd dimensional consciousness and moves into 4th and 5th. How long this will take is hard to predict, but the process is already under way."

"Can you explain more about the 4th and 5th dimensions?" one of the adolescents asked.

James nodded. "The 4th dimension is a higher vibration or faster frequency. To experience it you have to raise your own vibration.

This vibration is closer to source and allows you to easily connect to both your soul and with other souls. It also provides psychic gifts, such as clairvoyance, clairaudience, telepathy, energy healing, and many others psychic skills. This will have a huge impact in the way people perceive life. In fact, most will have a new desire to only create that which is in harmony and joy. The dark side of life will slowly fade away."

"The 5th dimension," James continued, "is almost impossible to explain with words. At this level of consciousness, you can literally manipulate matter and transcend time. For instance, if you want to travel somewhere, all you need to do is think where you want to go. You will instantly appear at your destination. If you want a house and all of the stuff to decorate it, then you can do it with your mind...."

"No way!" one of the adolescents exclaimed.

"When you think of the 5th dimension," James said, "remove all limitations that you can think of. On this level we have the ability to create what we want. One of the nice things to look forward to is that you no longer have to worry about energy or transportation, or even food. Eating is optional, but if you want to eat something you can manifest it.

"I have my doubts we will see anyone with 5th dimensional abilities anytime soon. In fact, I think there will be two timeliness, whereby the current Earth will remain in the 3rd and 4th dimensions, and a new Earth is created in the 5th dimension. Thus, there will be two planets. Some of us will ascend to this new planet, and others will remain behind.

"In the 5th dimension, we exist as light bodies. It is the same as it was during the early days of Lemuria. This is how this planet began and how it will end. There will be humans on this planet for another 6,000 years, and then it will return to a planet of plants and animals. It will become a paradise in perfect harmony."

One of the teenagers clapped. "This is what I have been expecting, but no one wants to listen!"

James smiled at her enthusiasm. "Well, it is your mission to make them listen. It is the job of the children of light to show the adults the way. You need to find creative ways to reveal your awareness. It is going to be your actions and behaviors that change the world. Whatever beliefs you choose to hold and how they manifest into actions and behaviors is more significant than you know. Never underestimate the power of being an example."

James stopped. "Okay, I think that is quite enough information for one night. Next week I will continue with this discussion, but I will take it slower and focus on examples of how the world is changing its consciousness. Then some of you in the audience can talk about how your consciousness and spiritual awareness is changing."

"Thanks for coming."

\* \* \* \* \*

The Pagosa Springs healing center and the next door community slowly became integrated over time. There were some who were not interested in the Gnostic spirituality that permeated both locations, but most of the people became Gnostic and followed their own beliefs and own way of spirituality. There was no single truth that was adopted by the community, and Charlene made sure that the freedom to choose one's own beliefs was not infringed.

The two communities began to integrate and work in each other's community. After awhile, it didn't matter where you spent your time, because you were a member of both communities.

Many of the children from the communities were children of light – advanced spiritual beings – and became healers at the healing center. The communities had several creative people who made products that could be sold and bartered on the Internet. Both the artist and writer also contributed income to the communities through their sales. It became a very vibrant and joyful place to live.

Animals were everywhere to be seen. There were dogs, cats, horses and goats. They even had a cow and some chickens. The cow's milk and goats' milk was made into cheese, and the chickens were used for their eggs and meat. They also farmed fish which people ate.

These two communities were not unique. Over time, they began to appear throughout the country. No longer was society able to support the urban and suburban lifestyles that was quickly becoming the old way of life. Jobs had become scarce and food shortages were common. People were literally forced to try a new way of life, and moving back to the land offered the ability to grow your own food. Plus, people were drawn to try something new.

America of the late 20th and early 21st centuries was steadily leading to the degeneration of society, and it was becoming glaringly obvious that a change of lifestyle was needed. There was an explosion of cancer, autism, diabetes, obesity, alcoholism, drug addiction, etc. You had to be blind not to see that our way of life was killing us. For this reason, there was a desire to try something new.

A change to a new way of life was inevitable. America was addicted to economic growth and a continued escalation of technology to make our lives more prosperous. This path was not sustainable. We kept buying the latest iPhone or other gadget, remaining on the merry-go-round. We didn't know how to get off. However, once the music stopped, and economic growth came to and end, we were forced to find a new way to live.

The small self-sustaining community was the answer for many. It allowed them to get off the merry-go-round of technology and to simplify their lives. It also provided a way to get back to nature, back to spirit, and into a more healthy lifestyle. And perhaps best of all, it created a sustainable model that could extend for generations.

\* \* \* \* \*

Mestos checked the timelines and was quite pleased. He mentally beckoned Sampson to join him and waited for Sampson to appear.

"We have achieved our desired outcome," Mestos said. "The mass ascension to the New Earth will take place."

Sampson appeared as a wispy light body wearing a white flowing robe. "That is excellent news. Others were expecting you to do another project."

"There will be one more," Mestos replied, "but it will be after the mass ascension. The volunteers have succeeded in their mission of raising the vibration of the planet to reach ascension."

"What about those left behind?" Sampson asked. "Is that what your next project is for?"

Mestos nodded. "There will be an opportunity for more souls to ascend to the New Earth over the coming decades. The new communities are having a large impact on spiritual awareness, and many souls are making significant progress. Our first three healing centers have led to many others. They will now multiply throughout the world."

"So the goal is to help as many souls as we can ascend to the New Earth?"

Mestos nodded. "Yes, not everyone can go to the New Earth, but we should help as many as possible."

"And what about those who do not ascend?" Sampson asked.

"The Old Earth will continue to raise its vibration and many will coexist in both the 3rd and 4th dimensions. As the vibration increases those who are not compatible with the new energy will die and transition back to the spiritual planes. I've studied the timelines and it looks like about 500 million will survive to build a new humanity. The good news is that it will be a planet of peace and love. This is the best outcome we could have expected."

Sampson smiled. "I will inform the councils of our success, and your coming project after the mass ascension."

Mestos smiled as Sampson's light body disappeared.

# Chapter Ten

# THE NEW EARTH

A few year later later, Earth reached its change point. The critical mass necessary for a mass ascension was reached. Millions of souls simply disappeared. One minute they were on the Old Earth, and the next, they were on the New Earth. This New Earth existed in the 5th dimension, where souls lived as light bodies. It was very similar to the Old Earth. The size was the same, with the same moon and solar system. All of the continents and oceans still existed, although there were noticeable differences. The coastlines had all moved inland from a planetary shift, whereby all of the continents shifted. The U.S. was split in two, with the Great Lakes connected to the Gulf of Mexico by a large inland sea. California was a series of Islands, and Nevada, Arizona, and Utah were mostly submerged by an inland sea.

The climate was now perpetually mild throughout the planet. The population was much smaller, and cities were built completely differently. There were no roads or transportation systems. Buildings had no need for elevators or stairs, or even insulation. The walls were very thin, and most of them were clear. There was no food production, because there was no need to eat as a light being.

The New Earth was a very harmonious place where souls could interact and live in perpetual contentment. Once you ascended to the New Earth, you had the freedom to choose what you wanted to do, and you could stay as long as you desired.

Those who did not ascend at the change point were left in a world that was still struggling to reorganize. The cities were still chaotic, and many had chosen to live in the newly created small communities. The economic systems throughout the world had broken down and forced economic growth to a halt. One benefit of economic hardship is the lack of funds for militaries. This caused military budgets and standing armies to shrink. There were still uprisings and civil wars in some of the developing countries, but the larger countries were no longer funding their armies.

People had to return to a much simpler lifestyle with less technology and less affluence. There was much less travel, and most people stayed close to home. Governments had shrunk and were no longer relied upon by most people. The healthcare industry had collapsed and was in the process of transitioning into new forms of holistic medicine and healing.

The energy vibration of the planet was steadily increasing. This was leading to a massive wave of illness and death. People literally were no longer compatible with the planet. This increased energy vibration also made it easier for people to tap into the 4th dimension. This made people much more spiritual and closer to one another. A spiritual shift was under way.

The Old Earth would survive, although the population would steadily decrease. The survivors would create a new civilization that was much more harmonious and spiritual. It would also be incredibly technological, with many people living in space. Futuristic ideas that originated in the 20th century would come to pass, such as advanced robotics, flying cars, and free energy systems. The technological leap would begin around 2040 when a great genius would make his appearance and herald in advanced technology.

\* \* \* \* \*

Mestos called Sampson telepathically and waited for Sampson's arrival. An instant later, Sampson appeared before Mestos wearing his usual white robe.

"Sampson, it is time for the final project. I would like to use the same council you used to build the three healing centers. Instead of explaining it to you, I would like to attend the council and tell them what is needed."

"Would you like to do it now?" Sampson asked.

Mestos nodded. "Yes, now is a good time."

"Follow me," Sampson said.

Sampson's light body disappeared and moved to the council location. Mestos followed his energy, and they both ended up seated at the council. Steadily the council members began appearing. They were seated in chairs around a circular table. They were inside a room made out of crystal with clear walls and a clear ceiling.

After everyone arrived, Mestos addressed the group.

"Thank you all for coming. We have one final project for the Old Earth that I would like to implement. There are two parts to it. The first part is to build an ascension center. There is only one place to build it, and that is in the Ascension Valley, which is in the state of Idaho, just south of Coeur d'Alene.

"It needs to be completed before the Earth Shift, which is only a few years away. After this shift, the energy in the Ascension Valley will allow thousands of people to ascend. It should be built and operated by a small group of perhaps twenty-five people. It won't be easy to find advanced souls, since most of them have already ascended, although there are some young adults who will be ideal. Tibus is the right person to assemble this group and build the center. He can select a few of you to help him.

"The second part is to help as many people as possible to ascend to the New Earth. There are many who were left behind who want to join their families. Find out who these souls are and bring them to the Ascension Valley."

Mestos paused. "Are they any questions?"

"Mestos," Tibus said, "the people who build the ascension center are going to want to ascend. Should I continue to re-populate the center with new people?"

Mestos smiled. "Use your creativity, Tibus. The more people who ascend, the better. I think this is something you will enjoy."

The group shared a telepathic laugh, knowing Tibus' obsession with helping planet Earth. After the laugh, there was silence as no one else had a question.

"I think we are done here," Sampson said. "Thank you for coming."

All of the souls began to disappear.

\* \* \* \* \*

Tibus used the same team who had assembled the group to build the Pagosa Springs healing center. It was much easier now that the 4th dimensional energy was so strong. All he had to do was find someone who had Lori Toye's Future Map of America.[25] This map had the Ascension Valley marked near a vortex in Idaho. Anyone who had passion about ascension and was aware of this map was a candidate for building the ascension center.

Tibus and his team found several candidates and picked Kayla. She was only nineteen, and perhaps too young, but she was a child of light and was obsessed with ascension and spirituality. Plus, she was a 4th-level old soul and a Queen of Spades, which was a very powerful card. Her karma and destiny made this a good match for her. Once she decided that this ascension center needed to be built, she would do whatever it took to make it happen.

Kayla was a social media addict and lived on Facebook, where she had over a thousand friends. She was looking for something to do with her life and wanted to get out of San Ramon, California,

25    www.IamAmerica.com

where she lived with her parents. She wanted to live in a spiritual community.

San Ramon was near San Francisco, and there were still a lot of affluent people in the area. Kayla and her friends wanted to get out of California before it turned into a series of islands. They had collected several maps of the future, including those by Gordon-Michael Scallion, Lori Toye, and Nostradamus (Dolores Cannon). They also had many prophecies that foretold of California and other parts of America becoming inundated by the ocean in a massive Earth Shift.

Tibus first decided to give Kayla some money. He made her a Facebook friend of someone who was due for a large inheritance. This new Facebook friend became a close personal friend, who lived only twenty minutes away. They began to hang out together, and both became obsessed with leaving California.

After her friend became rich, they found their ticket out. They looked on Lori Toye's map for a place to move. Kayla felt drawn to the Ascension Valley in Idaho. She told her friend that it was really the only choice if they wanted to ascend to the New Earth. They agreed to build their new spiritual community in the Ascension Valley.

Tibus found them eighteen friends who were ready to join them. Kayla and her friend bought two large motor homes and told their families that they were moving to Idaho to live. The group was very young, with most being in their early twenties. They were all single and had a lot in common. Kayla picked them and used her judgment. She wanted people with a good heart, who were kind and compassionate. And because Kayla was a happy person, she wanted people who were happy. This was a group that laughed a lot. They were also exceedingly intelligent. They would have no trouble figuring out how to build a small community.

Once they arrived in the Ascension Valley, Tibus took them to the location that he had picked. It was on twenty acres, which wasn't that big, but it had a large house built on the property. The property was for sale and had electrical power and running water from a well. The house was large enough to hold nearly all twenty of them with its six bedrooms and large kitchen. Once they moved in, they could add a few more cabins.

Once Kayla looked at the property, she *knew* it was perfect. Little did she know that Tibus had made sure she had that emotional reaction. The group was being guided from the other side, and was blessed and protected.

The energy of the Ascension Valley was powerful, but it was not yet at its height. It would magnify in vibration after the Earth Shift. The shift would occur in three stages over a short period of time. The first stage was actually to be a warning, when a small chunk of land in Southern California would be taken by the sea. After this event, millions of people would leave California, recognizing what it foretold. The second stage was a massive seismic event that would leave California as a series of small islands. Then the final stage would leave most of the western U.S. inundated by ocean. This final stage would also create a vast inland sea that would span from the Great Lakes down to the Gulf of Mexico. All of the coastlines would move further inland, with New York City submerged.

Once the group had moved into their new house, they began to change in subtle ways. They began to have a much closer affinity to one another, and love became a very powerful emotion that was shared among them. There were ten women and ten men, and several of them would form relationships.

Kayla was the leader, and she organized how they would build the community. She also formed a morning meditation group and constantly reminded everyone that this was a sacred place. It wasn't long before they began to recognize that they should understand the ascension process and what was required. None of them would ascend until after the Earth Shift, which was several years away. But they would begin their preparation and spiritual journey of reaching ascension.

\* \* \* \* \*

During the time before the Earth Shift, the ascension center became a dynamic place with a lot of activity. It now included more than a dozen buildings and sleeping cabins. There were several greenhouses where they grew most of their food. The number of people living at the center had nearly doubled, and now there were a few children and older adults. The small community liked to hike, rock climb, hunt, fish, and travel. There were young and full of energy and were constantly finding things to do together.

Spirituality was an integral part of the community. Kayla built a meditation and yoga room. She also built an ascension room that was a small ten by ten foot room with a large copper pyramid. The pyramid was large enough to sit underneath, and it had many small crystals glued to the copper frame. A large number of these crystals were selenite, which is conducive to connecting to your soul.

There were also specific crystals located in specific locations of the room to create an energy vortex. It was decorated to create an intense feeling of reverence. All of the walls were nearly full of mystical paintings and photographs. There was an altar that was full of crystals, including a large crystal bowl for sound vibration, and an incense holder. The walls were insulated to make it as soundproof as possible. This is where members of the community could come to meditate in silence, or to the sound of soothing music.

Kayla was intent on ascending. She created a weekly ascension group who studied the process of ascension. They would meet and share information about what they were reading in books and on the Internet. They also shared what they were personally doing for their spiritual journey. Some of them shared dreams and out-of-body experiences that they were having.

One of the members channeled, and he would channel once a month. The information that came through was helping them to understand the ascension process and their spiritual journeys. The channel also informed them that the Earth Shift was nearing and that this would usher in new energy that would allow ascension to be possible for many souls.

What the community learned about ascension was that it required a higher soul vibration, and that this vibration could only be reached by seeking a higher truth. This higher truth could be found using a spiritual path. The basis of this spiritual path was to grow closer to their divine nature.

The question that each aspiring ascension candidate must answer is: How does one get closer to their divine nature? This is a higher calling, a higher path that must be taken. Thus, our lower nature, our ego, must be shed and released. In the ego's place must arise our spirit, our higher self. This is where we can reclaim our personal power and be led from within. This is the path of self mastery and is not easily achieved. It requires a lifestyle change and discipline. The key is intent and desire, and to live each moment with this passion. This is Christ's passion, and must also become your own. Ultimately, if you are successful, you will learn to release your fear and move into trust. At that moment, you will be ready to ascend.

So the end goal is to know and trust that you are an all-powerful eternal soul. So powerful, that you can make your body disappear by increasing its vibration. Once you hold this energy within, you can meditate and literally vibrate off this planet.

\* \* \* \* \*

When the Earth Shift came, many members were ready for ascension. They were giddy with excitement. Who would ascend first? They had been working diligently on their spiritual paths and were ready. The ascension room was a busy place. They had to create a signup list and limit meditations in the ascension room for one hour at a time. The meditation room was also a busy place, with Kayla holding her morning meditations.

It wasn't long before people started disappearing – ascending. One of those was Kayla. She immediately came back through the channeler. Everyone was excited to hear from her. She explained that it was wonderful on the other side and that they had the option of going to the New Earth. The communication from Kayla created inspiration for the others who wanted to ascend.

News of what was happening at the ascension center soon found its way to the Internet and quickly spread throughout the world. It wasn't long before visitors began to arrive. Many of the visitors were not ready to ascend, but just wanted to see where it was happening and to be a witness. They wanted to talk to the people and find out how it worked.

The ascension center could have charged money and made a fortune, but instead they accepted donations. Their entire twenty acres were soon full of buildings and sleeping cabins. It was a hub of activity. Nearly half of the original members were still around and ran the place. In many respects, it was like a monastery. Those who came to live there had one intention: to ascend. They understood what was required to raise their vibration, and how it was achieved. Many had gone before them and had set a trail to follow.

There were now many teachers at the center who held seminars on the ascension process. Often these teachers would teach for a period of time and then leave behind a DVD or writings before they ascended. In the main building, there was a wall of pictures of people who had ascended. Many of them had left behind writings of what they had done prior to their ascension.

It was not long before more than a hundred people had ascended, and the number steadily increased to more than a thousand as more people arrived. The center became famous and a gateway for not only leaving the planet, but doing it in a manner that was the spiritual equivalent of graduation. Those who ascended achieved something that was very rare. No longer did they need to incarnate into the 3rd dimension. They were now free to explore the higher dimensions.

Pilgrims from all over the world came here to ascend. In order to make room for new visitors, there was a rule that you could only stay for three months inside the community. If it was not your time to ascend, then you had to move on. This created a lot of turnover. People were constantly coming and going. Word also spread that if you were not ready to ascend, then it wouldn't happen. It was recommended not to visit unless you thought you were ready.

After a while, it became perhaps the most sacred ground on the entire planet. Those who came to the Ascension Valley and lived at the ascension center knew why they were there. These were advanced souls who had a very close connection to spirit. And because the 4th dimension was now so prevalent, the degree of connectedness and affinity that the occupants felt for each other was profound. Everyone felt like they were part of a family and that they belonged. If there was a place on Earth where you could experience a simulation of Heaven, this was possibly it.

After a few years, the number of visitors slowed, and it was no longer a swarm of activity. It will still just as peaceful and sacred, but most of the advanced souls had already made their journey. The center began admitting one person per week, instead of one person per day.

\* \* \* \* \*

The healing center at Pagosa Springs had room for many newcomers after the mass ascension. Charlene and Margie were gone, along with many of their friends. Several people from the community next door were ready to move to the healing center and take up their work. It wasn't long before the healing center was operating as if no one had left.

For the years leading up to the Earth Shift, the healing center continued to heal people. The economic system did not recover, and healthcare had been decimated. The healing centers filled the void, and holistic and energetic healing became the norm. It was a period of stagnation, where economic advancement was very slow. It was a period of deceleration where everything slowed down.

Once the Earth Shift occurred, there was an influx of new people from the widespread dislocation. The water inundations impacted nearly every state. There were some places that were better off, such as Colorado, Idaho, Montana, Wyoming, and the Dakotas. These states had a large influx of the survivors.

The Earth Shift literally changed the world. If the world was in a period of deceleration leading up to the Earth Shift, then after, it became a period of tumult. Governments disappeared and people and communities were on their own. Power systems and energy grids failed. Water supplies and sewer systems failed. Even the Internet was down in many parts of the world after the Earth Shift. It required several years to rebuild the Internet, which was pieced back together.

Civilization slowly came back to life. Cities began to rebuild. Omaha, Nebraska became both the financial hub and government center of the nation. A smaller population survived both the Earth Shift and the increased vibration of the planet from the new crystalline grid. Those who survived were a more advanced race, with new DNA and a higher calling.

\* \* \* \* \*

After the Earth Shift, news spread about the Ascension Valley in Idaho. Connor decided that he wanted to go there and try to ascend. He borrowed one of the healing center's cars and took off on a road trip.

When he arrived, it was a busy place. It was much larger than the healing center in Pagosa Springs. There were buildings and cabins densely built over a twenty-acre area. It seemed as if all of the ground was being used, and there were very few open areas. Connor estimated there must have been at least one hundred buildings and cabins. Most of the cabins were small and located next to each other in neat rows.

Connor parked his car and found the main building. He walked into the entrance and found what appeared to be a check-in area. There was a long counter and two girls on the other side waiting to help.

"Hello," Connor said, "I just drove in from Colorado. I came from the Pagosa Springs healing center, where I have been living for many years."

"Welcome," said one of the girls with a smile. "Did you come to ascend?"

Connor nodded. "Yes, I did. Is there a place where I can stay?"

The same girl smiled. "Yes, we have some empty cabins. Did anyone tell you how we operate?"

"I read the information on your website," Connor replied. "I know I only have three months and that you do not charge a fee."

"That is true," the girl said, continuing to smile. "However, we do accept donations. We require that everyone who lives at the center attends an orientation. This lasts about an hour. We have one every night at 7 p.m., unless there are no new guests." She pointed to her right. "They take place right down that hallway."

Connor smiled. "I'll be sure to make it tonight."

"Perfect," she replied. "All you need now is a place to stay."

She turned and grabbed several keys off of the wall. "Molly, I'm going to find him a cabin. I'll be back shortly."

She then proceeded to head towards the door. "Come on, follow me."

She went outside and walked toward the center of the complex. "We could take your car, but driving is discouraged. As you will find out tonight in the orientation, it is preferred that you walk inside the center. People are often meditating in their cabins, and they prefer that it's quiet.

"But this is not a monastery. We still talk and have fun. There are no rules for silence. The car thing has been in place for a long time. It is kind of a tradition around here. We like to walk. It also has something to do with staying grounded."

After a short walk, she stepped onto the porch of a cabin and opened the door. She went inside and he followed her in.

"This one is open. What do you think?" she asked.

"Looks good to me," Connor said. It was a basic mountain cabin, with wooden floors and wooden walls. The furniture was just as basic.

She smiled. "Excellent. You came at the right time of the year. Late spring is when we get our best weather. Okay, then. I'll see you at 7 p.m."

She turned and walked out.

* * * * *

At the orientation, they learned where to get their food, where to wash their clothes, and who to call if they needed anything. The cabins had a radio system that connected them to the front desk. Unlike at Pagosa Springs, the occupants had to cook their own food. There was no kitchen or restaurant on the premises.

Instead, there was a location that held food supplies, as well as other supplies that visitors might need.

The speaker at the orientation spent most of the time explaining how the ascension process worked. Guests were given a booklet that had been created by Kayla and the original occupants of the center. The booklet explained what method they used successfully. There was also a library full of material that had been accumulated over the years. Each guest was to find their own way to ascend. There were no rules or gurus to follow. You had three months to do it on your own.

Basically, the center provided food and shelter for three months to anyone who thought they were ready to ascend. If they succeeded, then they would leave the planet in a state of bliss. If they could not ascend, then they could come back a year later and try again.

One benefit the center enjoyed was that people often left behind a financial gift after they ascended. People would often arrive with a sum of money and then leave it to the center after their ascension. This left the center with a large endowment to continue its work.

*　*　*　*　*

For the first week, Connor acclimated himself to his surroundings. He read some of the ascension material and walked around the premises. He met several people on his walks and found out that there was a group that was meeting at night to discuss ascension.

He attended these meetings and began to become comfortable with why he was there. He knew that he was going to have to meditate for long periods of time to get closer to his soul. He had never done this before, and he needed some time to get motivated. His job at the healing center was that of a manager and handyman. He was an old soul, but he had never found the need to meditate, other than on those occasions when he meditated with groups of people.

After three weeks of meeting with this group, he began to meditate four hours a day. When he wasn't meditating, he constantly read ascension material. His only break away from his focus on ascending was to go for long walks. It didn't take long before he felt a new closeness to his soul. He began to feel as if he were living in a strange place where his body was alien to his spirit. He could literally feel the difference between his soul and his body, and he chose to focus on his soul.

By the beginning of the second month, he began to lose his focus on reality. He became dreamy and felt that life was a dream world. When he came out of his long meditations, he had trouble remembering to eat. If a family member or an old friend would have visited, they would have thought he was losing his mind.

He decided he was ready. He walked down to the check-in building and signed up for the ascension room. He reserved one hour a day for the next four days. This is what was recommended once you felt ready.

The first time he went into the ascension room, he could not meditate. The energy was so powerful in the copper pyramid that he just wanted to sit and feel it. He also wanted to experience the same room where thousands before had ascended. He knew that he had progressed to the point where it could happen. In fact, he was confident that if he went into a deep trance that he would ascend in this room.

The second day, he entered the ascension room ready to ascend. He immediately went into a deep trance. He left his body and was met by his spirit guide. At first he thought he had ascended, but his spirit guide told him that he had not, and showed him where his body was currently meditating. He made the mistake that many make when trying to ascend. He had to go back, but next time bring his entire body with him.

On the third day, he ascended. He laughed when it happened, because it was so easy. It was like putting a key in a lock; only the lock was his consciousness. All you had to do was go to a specific place in your mind, and a pathway opened up. He saw the pathway and went through it.

He felt like he was having an out-of-body experience, only this time he knew that it was different. He could tell that he no longer had a tether back to his body. He was free. The first thing he thought of was Charlene and the New Earth. He immediately concentrated on Charlene and asked to be taken there. He knew that his soul would do as he desired.

Before him, he saw Charlene and Margie who were smiling. They looked like their old selves. Connor looked at his hands, and he could see that he had a human body. However, he could sense that it was much lighter and of a much higher vibration.

They were standing in a place with green rolling hills with oak trees, a small river, and birds singing. It was very scenic and beautiful. The sky was bright blue, and the weather was perfect.

"Connor! You made it!" Charlene said telepathically.

"Yeah, I went to the Ascension Valley in Idaho. I missed you guys so much that I had to try to find you."

"Oh, this is wonderful," Margie said.

Charlene laughed. "That must have been difficult. You never liked meditating."

Connor smiled. "You know me too well. Yeah, it was like going to the dentist. I didn't want to go. Eventually, I knew that was the only way to find you."

"Well, we are excited to have you here!" Margie said.

"Is it everything we expected?" Connor asked.

"Oh, yeah," said Charlene smiling. "It's paradise. We can go wherever we want, do whatever we want. There is no time here, or distance. Everything is quantum. You will learn what that means very quickly."

"Quantum?" Connor asked. "You mean everything can exist in multiple places at once? Kind of like a hologram? And that you can move to another location instantly?"

Charlene laughed. "I think you get it."

"So, it's a quantum reality?" Connor asked. "Plus, I can manifest whatever I desire?"

"Pretty much," Charlene said. "It's very close to living on the spiritual planes. The only big difference is that you can only travel around the New Earth. You can't take your light body and do interstellar travel and be superman. You can do inter-dimensional travel, which is how you got here. You can even go back to your soul group on the spiritual planes."

"No," Connor said, "I want to stay here and be with you for a while."

"That is fine with us," Charlene said. "We live in a small community inside a large crystal complex. There are only about a hundred of us. Come along, and we will take you there. Follow our energy."

Charlene and Margie disappeared.

Connor followed them and ended up inside a complex that looked like a very large building made out of glass. They were surrounded by tall glass walls and a high glass ceiling. On the outside, they could see rolling green hills and blue sky.

"This is where we live," Charlene said. "There is plenty of room for you. We are currently working on a project to help clean up the pollution on the Old Earth. We have an inter-dimensional spaceship, and we travel to the Old Earth to help them. You can join our team."

Connor smiled. "Perfect. Another project for us. Count me in."

They smiled and looked at each other, amazed that they were back together.

Charlene leaned her head to the right. "Come with us. We'll show you the grand tour."

www.ingramcontent.com/pod-product-compliance
Lightning Source LLC
Chambersburg PA
CBHW070034120726
47909CB00003B/1149